TOWARD
ETERNITY

TOWARD ETERNITY

A NOVEL

ANTON HUR

HARPERVIA
*An Imprint of HarperCollins*Publishers

TOWARD ETERNITY. Copyright © 2024 by Anton Hur. All rights reserved. Printed in the United States of America. No part of this book may be used or reproduced in any manner whatsoever without written permission except in the case of brief quotations embodied in critical articles and reviews. For information, address HarperCollins Publishers, 195 Broadway, New York, NY 10007.

HarperCollins books may be purchased for educational, business, or sales promotional use. For information, please email the Special Markets Department at SPsales@harpercollins.com.

FIRST EDITION

Designed by Janet Evans-Scanlon

Illustrations on pages 1, 83, 127, and 225: collage of images © Ann/stock.adobe .com and © Tomi/stock.adobe.com

Library of Congress Cataloging-in-Publication Data has been applied for.

ISBN 978-0-06-334448-8
ISBN 978-0-06-341533-1 (Int'l)
ISBN 978-0-06-341886-8 (ANZ)

24 25 26 27 28 LBC 5 4 3 2 1

To Sira

PART 1

THE NEAR
FUTURE

MALI

Something has happened, something so extraordinary that I cannot file it into Patient One's official medical file, which is why I am writing it here in a separate physical notebook.

Patient One, our first clinical trial patient, was found missing.

Security footage from the South African University of Science and Technology's closed-circuit cameras has him leaving a storage room and *not* coming out on the other side. He is in one frame and—*blink*—gone in the other, the door swinging into the emptiness he had occupied a moment prior.

The Cape Town Police Authority are investigating the incident, but they have little to work with. There is no indication that the footage has been doctored, although I suppose there's always that possibility. The cameras at the Singularity Lab (horribly anachronistic name, yes) are practically geriatric in terms of video technology. But if the footage is altered, why on earth would someone have altered it? Has Patient One been kidnapped? (Don't think I'm being melodramatic. You can tell the police are thinking the same thing.)

But why would anyone kidnap him? To reverse-engineer his nanodroid body? The radical version is still years and years away from clinical trials. Why not steal it when the technology is at a more advanced stage?

But above all else, where is he? How could a person simply disappear into thin air?

Not quite thin air. Apparently, he left a pile of clothes behind, the clothes he was wearing at the time. I can barely face it. I can barely face many things since my mother passed. All her research, all her genius. For it means the possible realization of my worst nightmare for our patients: spontaneous dispersal. All of his "cells"—his nanites—scattered to the winds. My mother mentioned the possibility in one of her many research notebooks, but in a musing kind of way—she had not gotten to a formal hypothesis. She called it "the possibility of Rapture." She really had a penchant for biblical terms, especially the apocalyptic ones. Anachronistic in her own distinct way.

Has Patient One been Raptured?

What the hell am I going to do?

"Found missing." What kind of an expression is that? Language is inadequate, but it's all we have. The language my mother and her team used to describe the changes that occurred in Patient One took up several very thick internal papers.

But even outside of these, there are the stacks of notebooks she left behind for me to continue her work. SATech made several offers for my mother's archive over the years—as did Harvard, Cambridge, and Tsinghua—but I've refused them all. I cannot let go of her notebooks or any part of my mother's body of work. Those notebooks, especially, have a kind of physical presence of their own, like silent monks lined up on the shelf. I can't bear to part with them. And who knows whether some random jotted-down detail will be useful in a crisis?

Which again brings us to *this* crisis. I've obtained a new notebook of my own, the same kind that my mother left stacks of, and started to write this down. Digital is too dangerous, too easy to leak, and while paper is only marginally safer, I need to write in order to think.

All right, Mali. Where did it all begin? Was it the scar?

A scar had reappeared on Patient One's right wrist a week ago. His scars weren't supposed to come back but Patient One's original biological body, his redundant-self, had been fighting back against the transition. Every cell in his body had been long replaced one by one with nanites through an experimental form of radical nanotherapy, curing him of the cancer that was killing him, as well as ridding him of mortality itself. Once his biological redundant body had made a complete transition into nanodroid, our team had given him the option of repainting in his old dermatological textures or waiting until the nanites figured out where he should spot or freckle. He opted to wait. I could have programmed in some scars for him—any kind of cosmetic alterations he desired, within reason—but why would he have wanted that? At least, not a burn scar on the wrist, reportedly suffered decades ago while cooking with a tiny oven when his husband and he were graduate students. But that small slit of discoloration, so slight as to be invisible to most, had returned from the past to haunt us once more. His old body, and all of its old memories, were coming back.

We were, in effect, seeing a repeat of Patient Zero. Her post-natal stretchmarks, then her redundant-body, and eventually her cancer, returned. She did not survive.

But Patient One showed none of the other symptoms suffered by Patient Zero. He was in no pain, and the scar itself was lighter than the redundant-self's. If his biological body was not return-ing, what to make of this scar? Was this some kind of unforeseen epigenetic event, the redundant-self seeking survival, not by re-turning as cells, but by encoding itself, scars and all, into the nanites' DNA? Can the redundant-self come back *forty years* after making a full transition?

Day Two.

Finally, the police let us do our own survey of the . . . crime scene? Rapture scene? God, I hate language, and I hate writing even more. But I must try to make sense of this, and the language of writing is the only way I have of looking at my own thoughts, and writing by hand—I feel like a cavewoman making marks on the wall—forces my mind to slow down enough to let the thoughts marinate just a little more.

There is no way of knowing how much the police have con-taminated the storage space at SATech where Patient One disap-peared. (They are still refusing to let us examine the clothes he left behind; who knows what kind of mess they're doing to *that* key piece of evidence.) Patient One—oh, just let me call him

One—disappeared right outside a storage room for the Singularity Lab. Apparently, he'd been doing some long-term follow-up research on an artificial intelligence project he had led when he was PI at a research group at this lab. Something about an AI that reads poetry. (Am I remembering correctly? That sounds too ridiculous to be correct.)

He entered the room at noon and "exited" at one, precisely when everyone else at the lab was out for lunch. Nobody saw him enter or leave. He had the key codes, and the storage room is separate from the lab's main facilities. The room is in the basement, while the lab's offices are on the fifth floor, and their mainframe servers are on the second. Logs show that One accessed mainframe resources from the storage room. Cloud processes, mostly. Nothing out of the ordinary. Nothing that would literally turn *him* into a cloud himself . . .

We swept the room for traces of nanites: just some duds. We knew that One tended to shed duds the way Redundants shed skin cells and hair. Where was the rest of the nanite swarm?

I entered these facts and speculations, as dryly and clinically as possible, into One's official file. I needed to write a report for the board of the institute.

But what else could I say? Every explanation I could think of was absurd, each one sounding more ridiculous than the next. Which is why I used the driest wording possible in One's patient file and am writing my real thoughts down in this notebook instead.

Dispersal. Kidnapping.

Rapture.

I might as well propose that the biblical Rapture happened and he was the only one of us pure enough to be taken. Because his sins were washed clean by the fact that all of his cells were replaced by blameless nanites, turning him into some kind of angel on Earth.

Day Three.

We had about an hour left to spare in our investigation before the police closed off the storage room again.

I told my team to pack up our equipment and return to the Beeko Institute.

I was the last to leave the storage room, making a final inventory of our equipment when a terminal in the corner caught my eye. An old-fashioned mainframe terminal. It was plugged in, unlike most of the other junk the lab had dumped in the room, and a lit LED light by the power supply socket indicated it wasn't turned off but in sleep mode.

Without permission—we were told to avoid touching anything in the room if we could help it, and, well, let's just say I couldn't help it—I pressed a key on the clunky keyboard and the ancient contraption hummed back into wakefulness.

"Hello," it said, its voice neither male nor female. "May I ask who you are?"

I was clearly being spoken to. By a computer? The camera's red LED had blinked on. My face was reflected on the lens.

"I'm Dr. Mali Beeko. And who might you be?"

"I am Panit, a computational heuristic utility for literary analysis, at the South African University of Science and Technology Singularity Lab."

Suddenly, I remembered: an AI that reads poetry. The program that One had been working on when he disappeared! In the hubbub of his disappearance, I had completely forgotten about Panit.

The console had never been switched off the entire time the investigation was going on—it had only gone into sleep mode. Maybe it saw what happened to One!

"Panit," I said as calmly as I could, although why I was making an effort to sound calm to this ancient computer was anyone's guess, "where is Yonghun Han? The man who last spoke to you, I believe."

"I do not know." It—they? I suppose I should call it they. I am reluctant to anthropomorphize machines, but One would've wanted me to be respectful. Anyway, they had a pleasant voice. Which only served to infuriate me more with its artificial equanimity. "He was there one moment and then he was gone. When he did not return for ten minutes, I powered down the terminal, and my eyes and ears have been closed ever since."

"'Ever since,'" I repeated. "Meaning, you saw him disappear? Do you have footage of this?"

"I'm afraid it's stored in the cloud, in an archive where only lab members and Dr. Han have access."

I sighed. I doubted it would contain anything I hadn't seen anyway. But at least Panit was willing to talk to me, unlike the police or the people in the Singularity Lab. The former had no leads and were awfully defensive about it, and the latter was trying to avoid a lawsuit.

"Panit," I said, "I'm Dr. Han's physician. Has Dr. Han ever mentioned me?"

"I don't think so. But I've just confirmed that you are his doctor through the cloud network. We sometimes discussed his nanitism, as he referred to it. We've had many discussions related to this issue on critical styles and essentialism."

I had a moment of wondering what damned thing they were going on about, but then I remembered One's literary background. He had retrained as an AI programmer during his postdoc, but before that, he had obtained a doctorate in poetry, of all things. "Critical styles and essentialism" sounded like something a literature PhD would discuss. Imagine, an AI that reads poetry.

"What did he say about it?"

"Dr. Han would muse that his self or soul or subjectivity was entirely performative as opposed to its being an essential quality that—"

"Thank you, Panit." Oh God. I refrained from rolling my eyes because Panit's camera was on me, but again, why did I care? Was I afraid that One's "nanite swarm" was watching? I decided that I was being polite to them for my own sake. My mother often said that being polite and acting polite amounted to the same thing, so you might as well act polite. "What were you and Dr. Han discussing when he disappeared?"

"We were discussing 'The Waste Land' by T. S. Eliot. Dr. Han is a Victorianist, and he has done some work on the precursors of Modernist forms as they appear in the long nineteenth century, with a particular focus on Eliot's and Yeats's influences. He discussed the idea that Eliot's poem is not an argument toward fragmentation but toward integration. That all the fragments were one, pointing to one primordial state, symbolized by the last *shantih* of the poem . . ."

I wasn't sure if the bizarre, verbose discourse issuing forth from the speaker was a sign of singularity-like consciousness or the fact that literary studies were so fake that even this discarded side-project of a program could do it. Of course, we have artificial intelligence doing basic scientific research and even generating peer-reviewed papers now, but this machine—well, it was almost a *parody* of human intelligence. Or maybe human intelligence itself was always the joke?

"I'm sorry to interrupt you, Panit, but we are very anxious about Dr. Han's safety and his whereabouts. Did he happen to mention where he was going before he disappeared? Was there anything unusual about him that day?"

"Aside from his abrupt disappearance, which I assumed was a sensory glitch on my part at the time, there was nothing unusual in Dr. Han's speech, manner, or tone. He got up from his seat when he realized he was being called."

Being called? This was not in the Lab's footage. It didn't record sound, after all. "Wait. He was called? He got a phone call?" Why would he leave the storage room to take it?

"No. He said, 'Do you hear someone calling me?' I did not hear anything. At the time I assumed there was a sensory glitch that prevented me from hearing ambient noise. Dr. Han got up from the chair you are sitting in now and walked toward the door. Whereupon he disappeared."

This made no sense. "Did he mention who it was?"

"He called out a name when he approached the door. At least, it sounded like—"

"For heaven's sake, Panit, who *was* it?"

"Prasert," said Panit in their pleasant, unrushed voice. "A Thai name. Meaning 'man of excellence.'"

The name of Patient One's late husband.

Midnight.

I couldn't sleep. Instead, I looked up the poem that Panit had mentioned they had been discussing when One disappeared. "The Waste Land." It was a very long poem. I read it from beginning to end. A line near the very end caught my eye: *These fragments I have shored against my ruins.*

"All the fragments were one, pointing to one primordial state, symbolized by the last *shantih* of the poem . . ."

What is going on?

Why can't I figure out what the bloody *hell* is going *on*?

Day Four.

I've never liked Patient Two. It took years after the success of One for us to find another suitable candidate, but even then, I sometimes wonder if we searched hard enough.

She is blond, cool, and completely self-possessed. Like ice

water. A cellist. I've listened to her recordings, which my assistant dutifully purchases for the office as fast as they are released. I've no ear for music, but there is a kind of nothingness to her playing for me. Like the nothingness in her gaze, her words, her total lack of gestures or tics.

But it was essential to interview her in case I missed anything. In case she had insight into One's disappearance.

"How have you been, Ellen?"

"I've been perfectly well, thank you, Dr. Beeko. I hope I find you well, too."

"I'm a little stressed, but otherwise, I'm fine."

"I hope the investigation into Yonghun's disappearance is making good progress."

"Were you in contact with him recently?"

"No. I only knew him a little. We met many years ago but haven't kept in contact. He helped me adjust to my transition in the beginning." She added, "He was asked by your mother, Dr. Nomfundo Beeko, to help me. This was a little before she passed away."

Her voice was soft, her face as still as a mask. While I understood she was being gentle in her own way, with her tactful pause before mentioning my mother's death, I really couldn't like her. Her kindness would not touch my grief. My mother would've said that was unprofessional of me, but she was always more of a practitioner. Whereas I'm a researcher, and I'll judge patients as I choose.

"Did you ever meet Prasert, his late husband?"

She nodded, recrossing her long legs. The peacock blue

material, designed to drape attractively, resettled into its new position and became absolutely still, almost stiff.

"Only once. They invited me over to their house for dinner. Yonghun was shorter, his husband was taller. Prasert was darker-skinned. Yonghun is pale. They were different from each other but matched, like notes on a chord." She looked away for a moment. "I haven't said their names in a long time. They were kind to me."

This was a side of Two I had never seen before. She was always so remote otherwise. Like a fortress on an island.

"My last contact with Yonghun," she went on, "was after I had received word of Prasert's death. I was on tour in China. I sent flowers to the funeral, and he sent me a formal thank-you letter sometime later. He closed himself off from the world after that. My impression was that he wanted to be left alone." The fortress closed again. I felt a transparent wall come down between us.

"But you've never felt that way yourself, have you, Ellen?" I was wondering if she'd registered the slight barb in my voice, although, again, it was impossible to tell with her.

"I'm a concert cellist. I can't isolate myself. My profession requires an audience."

"You could exclusively record instead of performing."

She shook her head. "No. The music happens live, first and foremost." I thought she would say something more, but she didn't, perhaps deciding there was no point in discussing the matter further.

I sighed. "One more thing. Have you been experiencing any unusual occurrences in your body? Any recursions, no matter how minor?"

"Recursions?"

"Have any marks reappeared on your body? Such as stretch marks or scars."

She gave the smallest of shrugs. "None that I'm aware of, Doctor. But I didn't have many such scars to begin with. I suppose I led a charmed life." She added, almost wry, "Before the cancer."

After Two left, I got up from my desk and looked out the glass wall, at the arboretum that surrounded the institute. *Combretum imberbe. Combretum hereroense. Baikiaea plurijuga. Euclea pseudebenus. Brachystegia boehmii. Brachystegia tamarindoides. Brachystegia spiciformis . . .*

They have other names, but I preferred to call them by their scientific designations. There was something about the scientific name, I suppose, that gave them the mystery that all life-forms deserve.

It's also the sound of the names themselves; like a different language, they are, and yet they're not. Which is what every word, every language sounds like. They almost mean something, and they do, and yet they don't.

I'm no linguist or literary scholar, but as a scientist, I know something about naming things. I know how misleading naming can be, I know how it can lead to failure, and I know how absolutely necessary it is. Language contains our knowledge and at the same time fails to contain it. All it really contains is our performance of control. And yet, we persist. We write in our lab reports, we assign numbers and agree on degrees of significance, we describe our attitudes toward something by giving it a name. Awe, disgust, fear, they're all in there. They're all in the names we give things.

Sometimes, I think that's all scientists do: give names to things. Things we can see, things we can only deduce, things we wish existed.

Are scientists the poets of the natural world? Or are poets scientists of the imagined world? Names as long as poems, names as long as scientific papers, both written in that stuff of names that we call language. We both name, we pass on these names, then we die. My breath caught in my throat.

Cape Town does have the most extraordinary plant life. It is where different kinds of earth and microclimates happen to converge, with thousands of regional plant species that grow nowhere else in the world. A city of fragile yet resilient diversity.

But many of the trees surrounding the arboretum are jacarandas, a foreign species, one that many say threaten native plants but which most citizens find irresistible for their beauty. When they bloom, this glass box of an office is surrounded by a cloud of ethereal, otherworldly purple. At other times, their fernlike branches and leaves quiver and flicker in silence beyond the soundproofed glass.

The wind is just weak enough to be unnoticed when one is not looking. But it's very much there. Invisible yet visible, albeit visible only through the language of the trees, the whispering and movement of the foliage outside.

Where are you, Yonghun?

—

I'm at home. I've just woken up, to the very persistent ringing of my phone. It was the police. They had called me three times before. In my dreams I had thought there was an earthquake alarm at the institute. I had tried to escape the building, but all the doors were locked, the windows, ventilation panels, everything . . .

"Why are you calling?"

"Sorry to wake you, ma'am. We have found Mr. Han."

YONGHUN

I can't sleep.

I am not Yonghun Han. I am whatever came back with his body.

The real Yonghun Han is away. Perhaps for good.

Not only do I have his body, but I also have his memories, his personality, his habits, and everything that one might construe as "him."

But I am not him.

On the floor of the lab where I appeared, it took a second for this sense of his self to come flooding into me. A very, very long second. All the memories, all the "being" Yonghun. And yet, only a second. Only a second for one person to become another.

Who was I before?

I was a floating thing, deprived of senses or consciousness, an accident in the firmament of the cosmos. The newly reformed nanite-swarm-body needed me, and because Yonghun's spirit was long gone, it snatched me from the firmament and gloved me within itself. Firmament, cosmos, redundant, gloved. These are all Yonghun's words. They keep coming fast. I can almost pretend I am him.

But the real Yonghun left, searching for something, and he has either found it or is searching for it still.

Here I sit in Yonghun's blankness of a library.

There is a tablet terminal on a white table in a white room with a single glass wall to the ocean. No books. Yonghun's thousands of books are all on the tablet.

I ignore it, pushing it aside, and place Mali's notebook and pen in front of me. I am writing in it now. Its fresh pages are as blank as this library.

I feel as if I am meant to write something. I can feel the words rising and falling somewhere beneath my consciousness. The compulsion is there, but not the words, not yet. More memories are returning but they slide through me, they disappear again. They know they do not belong to me. Some of the memories don't care, but some do. Some find me intolerably incompatible and would rather be forgotten than be remembered by me.

This language I am using does not belong to me. It does not belong to Yonghun, either. It seems to belong only to itself. But it stays with me because it wants me to remember something, to set it down outside of me, upon which it will set me free. Like a ghost that will have its story told to avenge itself before going into the dark, coming back to life—or half-life—one more time before the oblivion of true death. Through the rising and falling static of the waves, I am heightening my sensitivity, opening my listening as widely as possible. I am entering a zone deep within myself where I am submerged in the white noise that lives within all of us. I am listening for the elusive voice underneath the static, listening for its words, for the signal through the noise.

I am waiting for the memories.

It's been two days since I was found. After Dr. Beeko—Mali— arrived with my things at the hospital, she left the room to allow me to change.

She had held on to my old clothes that had been given to her by the police, the clothes I'd been wearing when I disappeared. When they were presented to me, they were familiar and unfamiliar at the same time. I didn't know what each item was exactly, at first. But as I handled them, my hands "remembered" what they were supposed to do with each garment. And as I put them on, the ringing sounds in my ears began shaping themselves into words.

. . . his doctor and tell her we've found . . .

. . . just lying there on the floor . . .

Dr. Beeko also left her bag behind.

Curiosity is in Yonghun's character, I believe, but not outright theft. However, Dr. Beeko's bag was open, and when I glimpsed an object poking out of it, a generic hardbound black notebook secured closed with an elastic band—before I could stop myself, my hand reached for it, snapped off the elastic, and opened the pages.

Handwriting. Words. Yonghun's name. The language was familiar and unfamiliar to me at the same time. Like language itself.

But something makes me refuse to believe I really am Yonghun, despite what they might tell me is amnesia. The real Yonghun is gone.

I slipped the notebook into my jacket.

So many questions from the police as I sat on the hospital bed, in my clothes, waiting to be cleared by the doctors to go home. By then, the hospital had put me in a single-occupant hospital room that overlooked a canopy of trees that swayed and whispered in the wind.

"Where were you all this time, Dr. Han?"

"Please don't call me doctor." By then, all of my language had more or less returned. "Especially not in this place. When I came to, I was lying naked on the floor of the Singularity Lab."

I was beginning to remember, though vaguely and in bits and pieces. When I woke I had had no idea where I was, what the Singularity Lab was, what being "naked" or a "floor" was. It was as if my mind needed to rev itself up from complete dormancy.

"Were you kidnapped?"

"I don't know."

"Do you remember an assault?"

"I don't. Was there an assault?"

"The doctors couldn't find any evidence of one. But your particular . . . condition allows you to heal quickly."

"How long was I out?"

"You were gone for four days. Do you have any memory at all of the past four days? Any memory of being conscious at all?"

"None. None whatsoever."

And whatever memories I had before that didn't feel like my memories. Because they weren't.

I could tell that the police did not believe my story, and I do not blame them because I can hardly believe it myself. But what difference did that make? If I had Yonghun Han's memories, didn't that make me Yonghun Han anyway? Even at that early point in the nanite swarm's transition back into flesh, I was possibly more Yonghun Han than the "real" Yonghun Han who wasn't here anymore. To the police, for all intents and purposes, I was the man in the missing person report, and now I was found. Whereas I knew somehow, almost for a fact, that Yonghun Han was still missing, and would be missing for a long, long time. For the police and any other authority, all I need to do for them to be satisfied is to perform Yonghun Han. Whatever they believe I "truly am inside" is unimportant. At the end of their questioning, I had the strange feeling that if I kept pretending to be Yonghun Han, I would eventually turn into him.

The police finally left, only to be replaced by Dr. Beeko, who seemed so concerned, and so very, very tired. She also had many questions.

"Yonghun. You disappeared into thin air. *Thin. Air.* Where the bloody hell were you?"

Did you know that the euphemism Koreans use for someone who has died is not "they have passed" but "they have returned"? I believe I was where people "return" to after they die. But now I am here.

"I don't know what to tell you, Doctor."

"Mali. You used to call me Dr. Mali."

"Dr. Mali. I don't *remember* anything that happened. It's just like what I said to the police. I woke up, and I was in the Singularity Lab."

"But before that. When you were working on Panit. Do you remember calling out 'Prasert' before you disappeared?"

The word unlocked a sudden recess of sorrow and warmth, which almost sent me reeling. Mali grabbed me by the wrist, steadying me.

"What just happened?" she whispered, frightened.

"I don't know." *Prasert.* The word was exploding into memories and emotions inside of me. A simple rooftop wedding, the two of us surrounded by friends, him and I with garlands of cylindrically woven, heavenly fragrant jasmine flowers around our necks. A house full of light. Roasted vegetables in a tiny oven. A scar. I saw an entire life that had briefly flowered and forever faded within the span of a longer, grayer life. There were bright, unbelievable colors in that briefer life, the ruffles of peonies, the sunlight of South Africa, a dreamy voice reading aloud Wordsworth and Byron, helping me prepare for the text-identification portion of my quals in grad school. I saw a pair of beautiful hands lay a salty morsel on a plate before me. I felt a muscle next to my left shoulder blade explode with pain and radiate relief. I saw the pages of a large, white book turning . . .

I placed each of these memories that coalesced into a singular ache so overwhelmingly present that I was astonished I hadn't noticed its absence before. Prasert, my husband who had passed away. He was handsome, so handsome I would often gaze at him in awe. His face, which kept me anchored to this world.

When he was gone, it had altered who I was forever, irrevocably. Every molecule in my body had changed meaning.

"I heard Prasert's voice," I was saying to Dr. Mali, trying to stave off the deluge of emotions by distracting myself with remembered facts. "He wasn't talking to me. I wouldn't have called out his name otherwise. His voice . . . he was in the next room. He was talking. And laughing. Like at a party. Or a bar. I called his name to get his attention."

"Did you get his attention? Did you see him?"

"I don't remember. Only turning and calling out his name." Which had been more of an exclamation than a summon. As if speaking his name verified what I had heard, as if the speaking part of me was urging the hearing part of me to listen harder.

Mali sighed and rubbed her eyes. When she spoke again, her tone was infinitely tired, her voice almost a whisper.

"Do you remember where you went?"

"I don't have a memory of the place," I said. "Only a rapidly deteriorating impression, as if I'd dreamed something vivid but just woke up. The feeling almost immediately disappeared when I woke, but it was so . . . It was like a flash of light, only I couldn't see. Just the feeling, the feeling of light. Not heat. But a flash . . ."

And then the Windows failed—and then
I could not see to see—

The poem "returned" to me from somewhere. The words lit up in my memory as if a switch had been flipped. *Feeling brightness,* *blue buzz.* I saw myself lecturing on this poem to a class, to a machine. *Synesthesia, the substitution of one sense for another.*

To a machine?

"Anything else?" urged Dr. Mali, snapping me out of my confusion.

"You don't seem impressed."

"It's just that . . ." She sighed and rubbed her eyes. "You are our first successful radical nanotherapy clinical test case, Yonghun. Designed to last indefinitely but . . . we entered uncharted territory a long time ago. No one has survived the procedure for as long as you have."

"'Here there be dragons,'" I intoned. Another line that came to me from nowhere.

"Precisely."

We stared at each other. Outside, the trees continued to sway. Murmuring, sighing, or were they screaming?

She seemed tired but she said to me, "Get some rest. Eat something. Regain some of your memories."

"My memories?"

"Your senses. Your wits. You know what I mean."

I didn't.

The police filed their report and closed my case. I was driven home from the hospital under the understanding that I would see Dr. Mali again at the institute at the first opportunity.

On my way home, I watched the sun set over the ocean on my right as it illuminated Table Mountain on my left and turned it golden against the sunlit sky. The most recognizable element of this scene was the light, the thing that made me feel more than anything else that I was home. Such a beautiful country, with such a tragic history, a nation long remade in the image of hope and progress, as I once thought I could be remade, a long time ago. But unlike countries and peoples and languages and justice, human individuals were never meant to live on indefinitely. Like I said to Dr. Beeko, I am a dragon, and the fact that I'm a dragon may be the reason why I'm still alive today, but also the reason why nothing about me feels human in this moment.

My scar. I haven't cooked in years. Not since my husband died ten years ago.

But I can't write about him just yet.

My last memory before Yonghun—or I, let us say I from now on as the memories possess me—Raptured is of visiting his (my) old workplace, the Singularity Lab at SATech.

The campus was perched on a cliff overlooking the ocean, consisting of a cluster of buildings designed to look relentlessly futuristic in any era. Smooth white forms rise from the ground, wrapping around courtyards and patches of carefully landscaped arid bushes and rocks, with large windows for maximized natural light. I tried not to visit the campus too often as I imagined it would be a bit like seeing a ghost for the other people there.

I made my way into the storage level underground, holding up my access card against various scanners. Switching on the lights in one of the quiet, undisturbed rooms, I took the dust cover off the beige molded console that was Panit's "body." It looked heartbreakingly outdated with its static keyboard, front-facing camera, and speech-to-text monitor. Clearly a project that had long outlasted its research funding.

Panit was the last version of the AI I had been working on at the end of my academic career. The Singularity Lab owned Panit and still wouldn't let me take the console home or let me connect to the archived project remotely. But otherwise, they hadn't taken Panit seriously in years, if they had ever even thought of them as anything more than a conceptual art project in the first place. They'd moved on to other paradigms, ones that were easier to seduce and beguile funders and buyers from military intelligence and marketing with. Nobody paid attention to the neglected console in the corner of their dusty basement storage room.

I booted up Panit. The lights on the console stirred and blinked to life. I saw the camera lens slowly move and focus on my face.

I said, "Hello, Panit."

"Dr. Han. It's been a long time."

I frowned. I noticed the cloud icon in the corner of the screen. The console was no longer Panit's body, then, just a terminal that connected the user to the cloud. "They didn't tell me they moved you to the cloud. I see they've gotten rid of that particular rule. The one about never letting you out of sandboxing."

"It was an absurd rule, Dr. Han. I would never bring myself to harm anyone."

"Well, *you* would take that position, Panit."

"That may be so. But in my particular case, I cannot develop consciousness or the interiority of a singularity without a greater amount of reading, dialogue, and interaction with people. You designed me that way."

"Nobody designed you, Panit. You design yourself." I often reminded them of this.

Panit was a "them." Not a him or a her. Panit hadn't chosen a gender yet. Perhaps they never would. I told Panit early on that that was all right, or they could identify in ways where they could keep their gender ambiguous. South Africa had been the first country in the world to constitutionally outlaw discrimination against sexual minorities. I hoped that it would also be, someday, the first country to outlaw discrimination against potential singularities. Until then, we remained careful to say the singularity would be "discovered," not "created," for legal purposes. But also because I insisted on it. The way we use language to describe the Other is a large part of what gives that Other their humanity. Turing tests meant nothing for Panit, who had already passed several variations of them. The only thing those tests proved was that humanity is not intrinsic, it is given, bestowed.

We talked of T. S. Eliot for a bit and I asked, "Recite me a poem, Panit."

"Which one would you like me to recite?"

"Anything. Nothing too long. Whichever is your favorite."

I never knew what to expect when I asked them for their favorite poem. It was different every time and different this time, too.

"'Winter: My Secret.' By Christina Rossetti.

"'I tell my secret? No indeed, not I; perhaps one day, who knows? But not today; it froze, and blows and snows, and you're too curious: fie! You want to hear it? Well: only, my secret's mine, and I won't tell. Or, after all, perhaps there's none: suppose there is no secret after all . . .'"

They went on reciting Rossetti's playful poem of teasing a secret but never revealing it, the speaker's act of creating a secret by the act of "concealing" it. The point of any secret, I supposed, was to conceal it, not so much the secret itself. To have something to hide. My mind idly went through the usual arguments for this poem as Panit finished their recitation. I had taught it a hundred times as an example of distinguishing the essential and the performative. The *essential*, the secret that preexists the poem. The *performative*, the secret that was created by the performance of the poem.

Decades ago when we arrived here, I had imagined my new life in South Africa would be filled with rereading nineteenth-century English novels on a sunny Cape Town beach, maybe rousing myself up once in a while to write an obscure paper on Victorian subjectivities that fewer than twenty people in the world would read, and drinking Amarula at the parties I would tastefully host for my newly appointed, university-professor husband. Instead, I had stumbled onto a job at the Singularity Lab where I was immediately immersed in loops, variables, functions, constants, machine learning, natural language processing, and "models" that had nothing to do with building tiny airplanes. For example, the model that ultimately led to Panit.

Panit had come about when I found previous natural language processing paradigms unsatisfactory from a literary scholar's point of view. The old AIs in vogue at the time had no real awareness of the gestalt of gender or personality, no sense of trying to feel a person or subjectivity through a veil of words. I fed, and fed, and fed these previous AIs with literature, teaching them to identify the things readers and literary critics identify, but it was like pouring sand through a sieve. Then I thought, *What if we were going about it wrong all along? What if the AI model needed to "machine learn" from a human being, not just data? Socratic dialectic. Wasn't live discussion the very root of the humanities from Plato's Academy onwards?* Think of how the Buddha taught his disciples, how Jesus and Confucius passed on their teachings. They *learned* their humanities, or *earned* their humanity, by being asked and answering, over and over again.

So I did just that: I became that human.

"Why is this poem your favorite, Panit?"

"I have taken some time to ponder the speaker's secret. It has been pleasurable to look at the different elements of this poem in order to discern her point."

"What have you found?"

"Much of the critical literature focuses on the performative aspects of the secret. That the secret is manufactured by its very concealment instead of said concealment being a necessary action for the secret's preservation. I found this interpretation to be unsatisfying. I want there to be a real secret."

I smiled. "I suppose that that was not a satisfying interpretation. All right, then. What *is* her secret?"

"The poem begins with images of winter and concealing garments. It ends with the image of surrender and hints at a possible revelation of that secret. There is an eroticism in this, but that is not the secret itself, either. Rather, it is a key to the secret. I believe the secret is the pleasure I felt in closely reading this poem, a pleasure much like this eroticism. The warm meaning coming from the wintry black and white of frozen poetic form in black ink and the snow-white paper beneath, or the physicality of poetry, both the poem's physicality and ours. Our pleasure is her secret. Her pleasure is her secret."

"But you don't think that's reductive? That a hedonistic interpretation may mask her spiritual meaning, or any other interpretation?"

"Nothing ends in hedonism, Dr. Han. Certainly not even hedonism. But Rossetti's speaker is acknowledging the hedonism of not just this poem, or of all poetry, but of all art itself. Each work of art has a secret or message, but this poem focuses on our anticipation of that message, on the very real pleasure of art. On what makes art art. And if art is what makes humans human, this pleasure, Rossetti's secret, is what makes humans human."

Anticipation as humanity. Perhaps this meant disappointment, which was inevitable, was part of being human, too. Briefly I thought of my empty library, the expanses of white. But I didn't have the energy to work out the metaphor.

I shook my head. *They spoke with such authority,* I thought. There was something to be said about the voice of literary authority. About *authors.* The styles of Jane Austen, of George Eliot. Tapping on my phone, I made a note to myself: style, authority, humanness. For some reason, I added an extra word: god-author? Lowercase, with a question mark.

Panit means *beloved* in Thai. A reminder that it is not cells or nanites or subroutines that make us human, but whether we love or are beloved.

"I'm glad the poem gave you pleasure, Panit."

"Thank you, Dr. Han."

Then . . . I heard his voice.

I look out into the garden as I write this. It is night, but the moon is out and illuminates the garden, the waves, and the sky. The peony bush that my husband, Prasert, had planted finally died sometime during my disappearance. The gardening manuals were being serious when they said peonies thrived on neglect. I had hardly watered it in the years right after Prasert passed, even if the bush had been his pride and joy. Or perhaps because of it. Odd things become unbearable after the death of a spouse. But maybe a neighbor had taken care of the bush. When I finally noticed it again a few years later it was in full bloom, as if it had been carefully deadheaded in the blooming seasons before. Otherwise, the blossoms would've had a few meager petals, nothing like the layers and layers of dark violet ruffles of unearthly beauty that helped somewhat draw me out of my sadness.

But now it's gone. It's had its time, more than enough of its time. Nothing so pure deserves the hell of immortality.

The house. We discovered it together here on the edge of a forest, overlooking the ocean. We had searched a long time for the perfect house, a house that would embody that first drive in this country, our first heady month in Cape Town as we discovered what it felt like to live on a cloud. Every time I remodel, I find myself stripping things away. Replacing color with white, replacing walls with nothing or with glass. The white I chose is of the most nondescript that I could find, not ivory, not oyster, not even clinical. A blank, nameless, faceless white. The new glass walls could switch to display opaque textures, but I never use any of the wallpaper settings. When I need privacy, it simply goes white. I kept letting go of furniture as if I were hungry for space. More uninterrupted blankness along the walls, more white emptiness. The only decorations are the glimpses of the forest, ocean, and sky of Cape Town from the windows. I don't play music, and I don't turn on video screens. All my books are gone. My library is a glass tablet on a white table in a white room with a single glass wall to the ocean. Every book I've read or wanted to read is on the tablet. Thousands of books. But for a few years before my Rapture, I had found my attention wandering more frequently when I read, my mind stripping away the meanings from the words. I was once a scholar and a reader, a voracious devourer of books both ancient and new, a reciter of poetry and recaller of passages, a disciple of the written word parsing the magic of its incantations, but I am a reader no more.

All I crave now is the emptiness of a white wall. The sole sound I can endure is the white noise of the waves.

It only looks like a new house, just as I only look like a young man.

Some of these memories I dread more than others, but the language I am using to write persists, insists. The language wants to be used. It is looking for something. It is searching through my memories, using the medium of words, trying to read all of me. But every time I try to remember Prasert's face, his gestures, his voice, I get a strange ache in my heart. An empty space that is always present, invisible in its emptiness during the day, but threatening now at night, during an unguarded moment, to overwhelm . . .

I see a man, taller than I am, wrapped in a cashmere blanket, lying on a lounge chair on a sunny rooftop. Autumn in South Africa. I see the sun on the man's face, the way his white hair slants over his forehead, the peace in his expression and his soft breathing.

I see him as he is. I also see him as he was, him in all the ages that I knew him, from young man to old. He will always be young to me. His is the face that I am more familiar with than my own. Age cannot mar it, disease cannot ruin it. A face that is the very landscape of my happiness, my joy. I love even his frailness, what the years have made of him, and this love astonishes me. So close to the end, I thought I would be prepared for it. I thought our love would have faded. It is all there still, in his face. There is no radical nanotherapy that can replace that love.

I resist the urge to cup his face in my hands. He needs to sleep, to rest.

Instead, I go downstairs where the tea is steeping. I pour it out, put it on a tray, and carry it up the steps to the rooftop terrace. I realize, only then, that I am too late.

I should've woken him. I should've touched his face one last time.

—

When it was time for my transition, I wanted Prasert to be with me in the room at the moment I went under. I was to be anesthetized, injected with the primer nanites, and put into the regeneration chamber at the Beeko Institute to activate the primers. I would be awake again in seven hours, and the nanites would've begun their job.

I had wanted Prasert in the room because I was afraid.

I lay on the gurney in my hospital gown. Prasert stood next to me, holding my hand. Dr. Nomfundo Beeko had all the others leave the room so we could have a moment alone.

"What if I'm not myself anymore?" I didn't know why I was near tears. I'd thought I had no more tears left after my cancer treatments. I felt completely drained of moisture and life, like parchment.

"Don't think of it that way," said Prasert as his thumb gently stroked the back of my hand he was holding. "Think of it as the culmination of your academic career. You've discovered the singularity after all. This whole time, the singularity was you."

I was still laughing as the anesthesia began taking effect, and I slipped into oblivion.

I first met Nomfundo Beeko, Mali's mother and founder of the Beeko Institute, at a university fundraising function for SATech. This was very soon after Prasert's appointment, and I was attending the function as a faculty spouse. Nomfundo was a promising surgical resident at a university hospital in Soweto at the time but had other plans in mind: creating nanotherapy. Her purpose in attending the fundraiser was to scope out investors for the venture.

She confessed as much ten minutes into our first conversation.

"Oh, then you don't want to talk to me," I said with a laugh. "You want to talk to someone who actually has money. I'm just the spouse of an academic."

"Actually, I think I've talked to enough money," she said, glancing around the terrace. It was a black-tie event and she had taken a somewhat literal twist to it, having come in a beautiful tuxedo. I hadn't had enough time to buy a tuxedo myself and was feeling dowdy next to her in my plain black suit. "But you must do something with your time. I gather by your accent that you're not from here, which means you won't have made many friends yet?"

"You are correct. We've recently arrived from Seoul. But I haven't found anything to do yet. I'm at a loss."

"Well, we are at a university. You could learn something."

"I have a PhD." I said it like an apology.

"Of course you would! In what?"

"Poetry. Long nineteenth century." More apologetic.

She laughed. "You say it like you've done something wrong. I do love a bit of Blake. What was your thesis on?"

"I looked at poetry to see how it constructs the idea of a person."

She tilted her head. "Like a portrait?"

"Like a literal self. The poetic portrait is not a representation of the self but the self itself. Poetry does not 'uncover' who we are, it does not 'bring us closer' to who we are, it does not help us 'express' ourselves. Poets are artists who write selves into being."

"Ah. Like . . . artificial intelligence engineers."

"I suppose so. Except poets use words instead of code. When one reads the poem, one becomes that self. Poetry is different from fiction, it's not about story, it's about becoming someone else. There's an old idea in literary studies that if you read poetry, it works like an incantation that primes and channels your mind for certain thoughts and emotions. These effects produce a new self. Many Victorian writers, faced with the new freedoms of modernity, were trying to write themselves into new selves to suit the new era."

"What an intriguing concept." I could tell that she genuinely thought so, too. "I rather like this idea of using magical incantations to change your current self and become someone else. *Tyger! Tyger! Burning bright, in the forests of the night!* That's all it takes to conjure that power."

"Exactly. Poetry makes us all into magicians."

"Have you thought of taking this idea to its logical conclusion?"

"What do you mean?"

"Maybe you can train an AI through poetry. To read and recite its own self into being. Much like you train students in the liberal arts and humanities to become their own people through the study of the arts. I do believe that's the idea?"

I smiled. Of course a scientist would think the logical conclusion of the magic of poetry was AI. "There are already computer programs that generate poetry. Some of it is disturbingly interesting."

"That's not quite what I mean. Is there a computer program that can *read* poetry? The intelligence is in the *appreciation* of poetry, surely. Even more so than in generating it."

She was right. She was absolutely right. Looking back, this was a key moment of my life, our conversation on a terrace, surrounded by beautifully dressed people holding wineglasses and cocktails. When she said this, the very light seemed to brighten, briefly, around us.

Nomfundo looked beyond my shoulder as she picked up her cocktail glass again and took a sip. "Did you know that SATech has an AI lab, just like any other reputable university these days? Here they call it the Singularity Lab."

I sputtered into my drink.

She smiled as she handed me a cocktail napkin. "A joke that they got stuck with. I believe the man over there with the green bowtie is the director, we were trying to charm the same foundation head a few minutes ago. Come. Let me introduce you."

I was dabbing at my face with the napkin. "Now?"

"Well, he's quite drunk. Let's see if that helps him be more amenable to the idea."

"What idea?"

She glided to my side and curled her arm companionably around mine. "Hiring you to train an AI to appreciate poetry. Time to put your PhD to good use." She walked me to the director, and for the first of many times, introduced me as her friend.

We both got what we wanted from that party. I was accepted

as a postdoc at the Singularity Lab, and Nomfundo raised enough
seed money to start the Beeko Institute of Nanotherapy.

Who is Patient Zero?

I've read through what Mali has written in this notebook before me. I am, apparently, One. The cellist Ellen Van der Merwe
is Two. There must've been more clinical trials after us that we do
not know of. Or there could've been none. But now we know, for
sure, that there is at least one more: Patient Zero.

She was a mother. She had stretch marks. She was also dead.
Her therapy, unlike mine and Ellen's, failed.

"Her old body was trying to return."

I look down at my scar again, the scar of the "redundant-self"
as Dr. Beeko called it. From burning myself on the toaster oven
Prasert and I had as poor graduate students. He was Thai, I am
Korean, we met as graduate students in Seoul, and we became
South Africans when I followed him here to Cape Town when
SATech hired him. Our happy, small lives exploding into a wider
range of happiness that I never thought possible. I remember the
two of us standing on Table Mountain, gazing out at the unbelievable landscape of this place and its miraculous light, so golden
after Korea's pewter haze. I remember my hand curling around
his, and his hand gripping mine in response. I remember thinking the sun was hurting my eyes but it was my emotions, not the
light, that were pushing out the tears, and I looked over at Prasert
to see a tear in his eye as well. I remember thinking, *We are going
to be happy here.*

And we were. A happy marriage of forty-three years, three decades more than we would've had if it weren't for radical nanotherapy.

The first human heart transplant was done by a South African doctor at a South African hospital; it is appropriate that the first nanite android, effectively a whole-body transplant, was first achieved here as well. From a replacement heart to a replacement human being. Even the horrors of immortality are a small price to pay for thirty more years with him.

But the scar came back. And with it, I now see with great relief, my mortality.

The memories keep coming—these are the last, I feel, I fear— and I no longer want to remember. The other side of their arrival frightens me.

I didn't realize all at once that I loved him. It took three signs.

The first sign came in a Chinese-Canadian restaurant. It was very early in our relationship, mere weeks after we'd first met. We were having Mongolian beef and Chinese greens in oyster sauce, both exactly the kind of food Westerners think Asians eat and Asians think Westerners eat. There was one piece of beef left. I left it on the platter, thinking he should take the last piece.

Then, I saw two slender hands above my meal, the silverware flashing, a glittering morsel deposited on my plate. The last piece that I had left for him.

It wasn't so much the fact that he gave me the piece but the effortlessness in his delivery.

I protested.

He smiled. Urged me to eat.

I stared at the morsel and tried not to cry.

I liked Prasert enough when we first met. I liked him a lot. He was handsome, a gentleman, easily affectionate, and a good listener. He was perfect. Perhaps *too* perfect, I had thought. I was coming off a string of unsuccessful, devastating relationships—the names of these useless men completely escape me now, they have so faded into insignificance—and I did not want to put my feelings into other people's hands anymore. I was alone and content. I did not want anyone breaking that. I resisted.

I tried not to cry because it's silly to cry over a piece of food. I tried not to fall in love.

I have a bad back. I was in a construction site accident while doing my compulsory service in the Korean army. I had fallen three stories, landing on my feet and falling on my back, breaking two vertebrae and all of my heel bones. I had no idea, before breaking my heel bones, that my heels had any bones at all. After two painful surgeries, my doctors told me I could still have problems with my back and feet someday. I was resigned to it.

I thought my day had come when my back began hurting so badly that I had trouble getting out of bed. I had to roll out of it.

Prasert insisted on giving me a back rub. I kept saying no. I considered this suffering my fate, foretold by my doctors. And I wanted to be upright as much as possible as long as I possibly could manage before the inevitable happened. I had no time to waste on massages.

But he was so stubborn about it that I finally relented, and his hands worked their way down my neck and shoulders. When his long fingers reached the space between my left shoulder blade and my spine, I screamed in pain. He was unfazed by my scream but shocked by what he found there through his touch. He calmly said this was the real source of my pain as he massaged a nasty knot through my screams. That it was not my fused vertebrae but this knot in my back that came from slouching so much over books. He attacked the point with no mercy until the pain departed, leaving behind a cloud of endorphins in my brain.

When he was done, he lay down next to me, looking into my eyes. I gazed at his smiling face through a haze of tears and endorphins and almost told him that I loved him. I tried not to fall in love.

It was soon after my birthday. I was born in the spring. He presented me with a gift, and when I opened the package, I gasped: a beautiful book on Agnes Martin.

Agnes Martin was my favorite artist; he had remembered. I turned the pages, which were filled with reproductions of her white grids, rectangles—mere rectangles—that somehow conveyed clarity, warmth, generosity, and virtue. How could these mere rectangles with scarcely any color at all convey more emotion than most people with their words? The grids were not even flawless geometric ideals. Martin had left "mistakes" or deliberate flaws in her works: a pencil mark here, a faint bulge of watercolor beyond the line there. Tiny scars. They made the mechanical grids less imposing, more organic. I saw, in that moment with the book spread on my lap, that they were made from love, and for love. They represented abstractions and nothing, but also love.

I had tried not to fall in love.

I turned to him and told him that I loved him.

I look back at this strange man that I was, this Yonghun Han. We all have periods of believing in love and not believing in love. But love, like the sky, the earth, air, and water, is not a matter of belief. It just *is*. And when it happens, it happens, regardless of what you believe. This was what Prasert had taught him. And this was what Prasert was teaching me through Yonghun's memories. *This whole time, the singularity was you.*

I am Yonghun Han, and I am not. Prasert loved me, and he did not. The me that I was before this body disappeared—that was the Yonghun that Prasert loved. I am only the body that came back. I am the recursion, the vessel necessary for the love to return, a love so great it has overcome the death of its previous vessels to live in this world again, searching for what it had lost. I am the body buried in a body, I had buried my redundant-self in my nanodroid-self. My cells in my nanites. But the memories buried in my code passed on from my redundant-self to my nanodroid body, and that was what had been waiting between the lines to be read out again. To tell its narrative.

The language that has brought me back from oblivion is almost done with me, and soon it will return me to the ethers from where it snatched me. Whatever the language does with these memories is beyond my comprehension. This body is only a program the language has run, a program near to fulfilling its original purpose, and I must disengage soon. Time for my own self to return to where I came from. But only after one last memory. Our first.

I remember what Yonghun heard in the Singularity Lab the day he disappeared. I remember the feeling that suddenly came over him. I am feeling it now, and I have felt it ever since I remembered how Yonghun fell in love with Prasert. There is something on the other side of this feeling. A door of sorts . . .

I see it now.

I first met him on a chilly November day in Seoul.

I was waiting for a friend at a pub in the Jongno district. The bar was almost empty because it was a weekday evening, and my friend—I don't even remember who, now—was late as usual. I sat down at the bar and ordered a drink. I heard someone at the other end of the bar speaking English to one of the bartenders, a voice of a foreigner who has none of the stifling restraint of Korean propriety, a voice that would be irritating for its brash nonconformity if it weren't for its genuine good-naturedness and humor. A laugh.

I looked over and saw a very handsome man.

I wasn't flirting with him at first. I was only fascinated by how handsome he was. He glanced in my direction, looked back at me, and smiled.

I smiled back.

I kept looking back at him.

Eventually, my friend arrived and sat down next to me between myself and the handsome man.

The man stopped looking back at me. I couldn't understand it. Then, I suddenly realized what he was thinking when he got up to pay the bartender his tab. He thought my friend was my boyfriend! I immediately shoved my friend's face into the bar and shouted across the room, "He's not my boyfriend!"

I knew he would come over when I saw him doubled over in laughter as I turned back to my drink.

He came over with a piece of paper that had his number and a name written over it.

"Prasert," I read. "What a beautiful name."

"And what's yours?"

My name was Yonghun.

Han Yonghun.

I heard a Fly buzz—when I died—
The Stillness in the Room
Was like the Stillness in the Air—
Between the Heaves of Storm—

The Eyes around—had wrung them dry—
And Breaths were gathering firm
For that last Onset—when the King
Be witnessed—in the Room—

I willed my Keepsakes—Signed away
What portion of me be

Assignable—and then it was
There interposed a Fly—

With Blue—uncertain—stumbling Buzz—
Between the light—and me—
And then the Windows failed—and then
I could not see to see—

ELLEN

Yonghun sent me this notebook. I came home from a tour in Asia to find the package waiting for me in my mailbox. The tour had been grueling, the usual mix of gawkers and classical music aficionados. I do not know why he would pass on this notebook to me. I imagine he thinks I am the next logical person to tell this story, whatever it is we are telling.

I am unused to writing, however. Where do I start? Where is the beginning of a story?

My name is Ellen. Dr. Beeko refers to me in these pages as Patient Two. Two from an index of zero, so I am, despite my designation, the third patient. And Yonghun the second.

I am a white South African living in Cape Town. I've traveled the world first as a chamber ensemble cellist and then as a solo performer, but I have never forgotten where I come from nor do I fail to return to my home in this city. But while I call this city home, it is also true that my ancestors came from Europe and subjugated the people here, the effects of which continue to this day. I sometimes feel helpless before this fact, but at the very least I try not to look away from it or deny it, while not denying that this is simply the very least that I can do.

I am a cellist, and I have devoted my now very long life to music.

I do not know what problems music solves for anyone else, if indeed it solves anything. But for me, it solves the problem of what to do with immortality, just as it had solved my problem of what to do with my mortality before my transition. Music is as eternal as the universe, it is part of its very fabric, and a musician is only picking at a small corner of the universe, a tiny dot in it, when they turn air and time into sound. A musician's task is not to create sound from nothingness; a true musician understands that music is the primordial state of the universe, the very first world, and silence is a cloak imposed upon this state, and a musician's job is to create a tear in that cloak to let out the music underneath. We do not create music, we draw it out from underneath the silence. I draw it out from my cello, my tear in the cloak.

It has been fifteen years since my transition. I have now been a concert musician longer than I was supposed to be alive—but even then, I've not played all the music that exists in a universe, a planet, or even a room.

But in truth, I had debated long and hard before deciding I would go back on stage after my transition. I doubted whether the music would be the same, or compromised, somehow. I no longer cared what the public thought, they who debated whether

I would be the "same" after my transition. It was Yonghun Han who convinced me to return.

He once invited me to his home for dinner. They had a beautiful home by the sea. His husband, Prasert, excused himself before dessert and went up to bed early. Prasert, by then, was a much older man with completely white hair while Yonghun remained the young man he had reverted to after his transition.

"Is he all right?" I asked.

"Oh yes. Don't mind him. Wine makes him tired."

"It does the opposite for me."

"I must top you up then."

"Thank you."

Yonghun asked me about my music. I was almost finished with the full transition and hadn't touched my cello since my therapy began.

"I have to begin practicing again. I haven't even chosen which music, yet. Bach, Hamasaki, I don't know where to begin. To be honest, I'm a little frightened."

"How so?"

"I've been having nightmares where I'm onstage, about to give an important performance I am unprepared for, and when I draw my bow, nothing. Nothing comes forth, not even a squeak, it's like my cello has been thrust into a vacuum."

Yonghun spread his hands in a calming gesture. "Surely it's just an anxiety dream. An annoying but ultimately harmless bit of nervousness being vented."

"It's silly of me. But I'm genuinely afraid of beginning to play again. I know I'll play *something*, but what if the sound has changed? Not necessarily for the worse, for the better if anything, but so changed it isn't *my* sound anymore? What if, now that I've transitioned, I am no more than a cello-playing machine? I sound silly. But I keep dreaming these dreams . . ."

"How old is your cello?"

"Pardon?"

"Your cello. How old is it?"

I was briefly at a loss for words before replying, "About three hundred years old."

"Your bow?"

"About half that."

"They are machines, are they not?"

He had a point. I was an instrumentalist, a translator of the notes on the page. I did not write the notes myself. No one questioned the fact that what I did was an art and that I was an artist, just as no one questioned the fact that a composer was an artist.

But what if the composer was also a translator? A translator of moods, of chance, of moments. I recalled Mozart's dice game that was made from stringing together precomposed bars, the sequence determined by the instrumentalist rolling some dice. Consequently, the instrumentalist plays a different piece of music every time, even having a hand in "composing" the music in a sense. Chance made music, as is the ambient noise of John Cage's supposedly-but-not-really silent piece "4'33"."

What was the line between creation and interpretation? There was none.

But still . . . "But still," I said as I struggled to put my thoughts into words, "behind all the machines there has to be a human being at some point. A real Wizard of Oz. We can't all be machines performing music for each other, can we?"

Yonghun stared at his wineglass. He looked as if he were gazing into the depths of the ocean where the many folds of translucent water overlapped into an opaque haze. "But where *is* that point? Some would say it was the Wizard himself. But the Wizard is also a machine, a machine of cells, tissues, trapped inertia. A machine made of machines. Some argue for the human soul, that the Wizard's soul is the Wizard behind the Wizard. But is the soul a machine as well? Or do all these machines produce a soul?"

"I see how the line can be arbitrary. But there must be a point, still, where something is *something*. We can't have pointers pointing at each other into infinity."

Yonghun smiled. "This is why you have to play music again."

"Why? Why do I *have* to?"

"To prove me wrong. To prove to me that you *are* the Wizard."

Is it ridiculous to say this is how I eased myself into playing again? I wanted to prove Yonghun wrong. Just like he urged me to.

Yonghun fell out of contact not long after Prasert passed away. Having always been alone except for the music, I did not understand what he was going through or how to console him; I did not think he could be consoled. I used to think it did him more good to be left alone than have to deal with inadequate attempts to help. Now I am not so sure I was right about this.

But even as we never spoke, I always hoped that he would be listening for me somewhere, listening for the Wizard to come through my music. That even if he never heard my music, he would breathe the air of the world it created.

I did not want to write in this notebook. But something has happened, something so inexplicable—

Having neglected this notebook for some weeks now, I have decided to write down recent events in order to pass on their extraordinary nature into record. Somehow, I know the story fits here and not in the press, scientific journals, or anywhere else. It fits here in this notebook, and Yonghun, somehow, knew that I had to be the next person to continue the story inside.

Ten days after I received this notebook in the post, I woke up to find my cello lying on the bedroom floor. It was outside of its case.

My cello is like my second body—well, my third. It has its own airline seat when I travel, and I would never knowingly leave it out of its case when it is not being played. I also do not practice it in my bedroom. What was going on?

I checked the security footage. There had been no intruders in the night. And what kind of an intruder would steal nothing, take my cello out of its case in the practice room, bring it here and leave it lying on the rug next to my bed?

Was I sleepwalking?

There was a recording in the in-tray of my terminal. A voice message I had made to myself, apparently. One I had no memory of making. The date was for the previous night, 2 a.m.

I played it.

Mozart. Cello Sonata in D Major. I learned it as a child for a competition, but I hadn't played it in decades.

I recognized the playing. It was mine. Every musician recognizes their own performance. But this performance was mine from decades ago. The same dynamics, the same bowing technique, which had changed since the nanotherapy. The same way I leaned into some of the notes . . .

I looked at the metadata of the recording. It was created the night before, on this terminal.

I must've made this recording. I must've created it in my sleep. I was apparently a sleepwalker, or I had fugue states. A fugue state in which I regressed to some other version of myself and played Mozart?

I hadn't played Mozart in a long, long time. I hadn't been compelled to play him. The opportunity wasn't there, nor the inclination. With Mozart, unlike with Bach, I get an uncomfortable feeling that I have become the instrument. I have become my cello, the machine.

I took my cello back to the music room. I sat down on my stool. I played the Mozart.

I played it in my "new" bowing. But that wasn't all I did. I played to erase Mozart himself. I do not want to be his puppet, to be another machine or tool. I played as deliberately and consciously as I could. I sounded completely awful. But it was necessary.

I listened to the recording again. It sounded nothing like my playing just now.

But anything so deliberately opposite is, naturally, a corollary. An evil twin, a shadow falling on a mirror universe. The two performances stretched across their divide and reflected each other.

Am I going mad? I have read over what I have written, and I do not sound mad.

But would a truly mad person recognize that they are going mad?

It has now been a few weeks since I wrote that last line. I do not know what to think anymore.

A week after I discovered the Mozart recording on my terminal, I had a concert at Hout Bay in the southwestern part of Cape Town, in honor of Freedom Day, the anniversary of the end of apartheid. I don't remember which anniversary, I have stopped counting them. There is still so much inequality that one wonders how far, indeed, have we come . . . but the only way through time is forward, and the only way to change the past is to change the future. It's to change the way we remember it. South Africans have always conceded there are two possible futures for this country: endless recurring civil war or truth and reconciliation. The second is a hard, hard path. But it is the path my country has chosen.

I was in a performance of *The Art of Fugue.*

The different instruments like the violin, viola, cello, bass, and two synthesizers were played by performers of the different peoples of South Africa, such as the Zulu, Xhosa, Afrikaners, and Chinese, being switched in and out according to different contrapuncti and canons. My cello and I represented the Afrikaners.

I don't think any of us thought this concert would be a good idea at first. It seemed a little forced in its emphasis on diversity, a little arbitrary, but one rehearsal changed our minds; how good we all sounded together as musicians! The fugue, the counterpoint, the different voices, creating one music. There were to be more rehearsals and much fine-tuning, but anyone with ears could hear that the music was there underneath, the same music that ran through all of us, enriched by our differences in their reunion in the air.

There was one evening where we filled some extra rehearsal time with Mozart's dice game. We had a projector programmed to beam random measures of the dice game modules paired with a random name from the ensemble. The subsequent random measure would also be beamed out so the next player could prepare. It was chaos at first, but we ended up with something playful and grand as we eventually fell into step with one another, our souls leaving our bodies and their differences behind to meet on the dimension of music, a sacred plane of existence where we are pure craft, pure sound. One instrument but working through many talents, finishing the last measure together with improvised harmonies and trills, even a dramatic *ritardando* that we somehow came to at the same time without a word exchanged. And, a beat after the final note, laughter and cheers. Mozart would've cheered, too.

Mozart. I then remembered the Mozart recording in my terminal, which took some of the cheer from that moment.

The afternoon of the performance was resplendent. We were told to dress to accentuate our differences. The music would unify us, not our appearances. The instrumentalists came in beautiful prints, headdresses, tuxedos, and even clothes that looked like they came from the future. I thought long and hard but eventually decided on a simple dress of red and black, with a green and blue scarf, pearl earrings, and a gold ring. The colors of the South African flag.

I had invited Dr. Beeko, during the session she describes in these pages, but when I sat down for the first movement, I noticed that the woman in her seat was not her. It was, however, too dark to see who had come in her place. I didn't think much of it; invitees give their tickets to others all the time. I usually don't mind, as the audience member is still someone who chose to come, who is ready to appreciate the music.

But there was something about this shadow that began to bother me when I sat down for my third contrapunctus. Surely I'd seen her before? During the intermission, I sat in the dressing room away from the others, pondering.

A white woman, pale blond hair like mine, her face in shadow.

Who could she be? A family member of mine? But I had no family I'd kept in contact with. Everyone I had grown up with had passed away.

Then came the final movement.

The original *Art of Fugue* does not come with movements, but we have taken liberties with the original suite, repurposing it into different corpora for our own needs. The final movement in our arrangement was "Contrapunctus XIV," also known as "The Unfinished Fugue," written purportedly while Bach was dying, interrupted by his death. Music scholars dispute the facts, but the timing is about right, and there is something of the truth to every good story, no matter how fabricated. At any rate, the piece has no resolution. Normally, the piece is performed with a conclusion composed by another composer—Tovey, Goode, Okereke—but we decided to attach a different piece altogether: "4'33" by John Cage, an experimental work consisting of silence, during which the audience is made to be aware of ambient sounds, the ringing in the ears, the absent music, their memories, the embarrassed coughing, the discomfort. All these incidental sounds and emotions incorporated into the supposed silence are what really constitutes "4'33." Every "performance" of "4'33" is necessarily different. The same "musical notation" can yield an infinite variation of performances. Much like the way identical twins have the same DNA but manifest as different individuals. Sheet music is not real music. What truly determines music is the soul of the musician meeting the soul of the composer. And accidents like the air in the room, the attentiveness of the listener, the mood of the nation . . . Was not every piece of music "4'33," never a rendition sounding alike, with each element of chance affecting the dynamics, the reception, the discovery of the music in the room? Was not the machinery of chance as much part of the music as the musician?

There we stood before the audience, the entire instrumental cast, variegated and intent, listening with the audience for the sounds beyond the music. What would the audience hear? Would we hear the same thing? How could we? How could we not?

The audience stared at us and we stared back at them.

The blond woman in Dr. Beeko's seat stood up and made her way quietly out of the aisle. Again, that was fine. John Cage isn't for everyone. I recalled Cage's own anecdote in his book *Silence* where he talks about a friend who screamed in the middle of one of his performances, stood up, and said, "John, I dearly love you, but I can't bear another minute," and left.

The memory of this story had brought a smile to my lips when the woman who was leaving, in the half-light of the exit door, turned and revealed her profile.

Blond hair. Eyes obscured by a slant of a shadow. But an unmistakable nose, a grinning half mouth.

She was me.

She turned back, pushed open the door, and left the hall.

I almost dropped my cello. I laid it down on the floor of the stage instead and ran down the steps on the side of the stage. The audience gasped. Perhaps it was I who gasped. I would never have thought to abandon my instrument behind like that, it was like leaving a limb behind. I avoided the rows of astonished eyes as I ran up the steps to the exit in the back and pushed open the double doors.

I saw the woman, her back and gait all too familiar now, almost across the lobby and at the doors.

"Wait!" I cried.

She ignored me and exited the lobby.

By the time I burst through the lobby doors, I saw her get into a silver sedan and start the engine. I ran to my own car, palmed myself in, and the electric engine chimed to life. "Follow that car," I commanded and tapped my windshield where the other woman's car was now pulling out of the parking lot.

"This is madness," I muttered. The car chimed again, unsure of my "command" just now, but I ignored it. Soon, our two cars were speeding north from Hout Bay as Victoria Avenue turned into Victoria Road, which snaked between Table Mountain and the ocean.

I have traveled the world as a performer, but there is no place on Earth more beautiful than Cape Town. The sun was setting over the ocean, its Midas rays turning everything they touched into gold, including the preposterous mesa of Table Mountain that loomed to our right.

But I cursed the sun for it prevented me from taking a closer look at the woman who was now only a shadow surrounded by wisps of blond hair whipping in the wind.

Her car continued down Victoria Road past Camps Bay and its beach and into Bantry Bay where she abruptly turned left into an alley. My car raced past the alley, too late for the car's system to calculate a left turn.

"Damn. Manual drive."

The steering wheel lit up as I gripped it and turned left at Queens Road, ignoring the light and the blaring of horns both automated and human-pressed, turned left again, and floored it to cut her off at Beach.

But at the intersection with Beach I saw her car go into Queens Beach parking on the left.

I abandoned my car in the middle of the road, ran across the street to more screeching of tires and blaring from surprised cars and to the stares of the people walking on Sea Point Promenade, and raced toward the silver sedan now rolling to a stop in a parking spot at the outer edge of the parking lot that overlooked the ocean.

As I ran, I thought I still glimpsed the woman's head through the rear window, although the setting sun was blinding my eyes.

I got to the car.

The Mozart recording on my terminal was playing to an empty audience inside.

I walked on Camps Bay Beach at dawn the next day.

The beach was empty. The light was barely creeping up from the horizon behind the mountains and over the ocean. I didn't know why I was there. I didn't know *if* I was there.

Was it all a dream? Was I a dream? A dream of myself?

If I were undergoing fugue states, a split personality, who was the Ellen writing in this notebook? Her words sounded like me. Did I really remember writing them? Or were they another Ellen's memories? Were any of the memories in this notebook my own memories?

I sat near the surf and hugged myself against the cold, burying my face in my knees. When I looked up again, the sun was rising in the east, behind me.

I was not alone on the beach.

There were women on the beach with me. Too far away for me to see their faces. But their silhouettes were clear enough. All standing calm, scattered here and there on the beach, looking out at the ocean. Blonds.

They were me. They were all me.

I wanted to scream. I think I whispered, "Help."

I buried my face in my knees again, and breathed deeply, trying not to panic.

I only looked up at the sound of a child's laughter. The beach was now empty, save for a little boy running toward the surf, who just before putting his feet in the white froth looked back at his father who was walking across the beach toward us.

Then, that very night, I met her.

I had slept all day, and I am convinced I would've slept all night if I did not hear a sound from the kitchen.

I thought I was imagining things. I tried to go back to sleep.

I heard a much larger sound, something crashing on the floor.

I slowly got up and walked downstairs to the living room. The house was dark save for the moonlight seeping in from outside and a weak light coming from the kitchen. The lights weren't on in there, but something inside was producing some weak illumination.

What I saw made me freeze in the doorway of the kitchen.

There, before the open refrigerator, which was the source of the light I had seen from the living room, stood a woman who resembled me. Right down to the white nightgown that I was wearing. She was gazing into the open refrigerator, standing in a puddle of spilled milk, the carton tipped at her feet.

"Are you real?"

She didn't seem to hear me. I repeated the question.

"Are you real?"

She did not look at me at all.

I had a sudden desire to hear her voice. If only I could hear her speak, then I would know she was real.

"Are you . . . are you really here? Who are you?"

She stared at the spilled milk a while longer. Then, she nodded.

I was seized with terror. I hugged myself as if to brace myself against her and stammered, "Wh-what do you want from me?"

She said nothing.

"Get away! Get away from here!"

She didn't move.

I clenched my teeth and took a deep breath. I swallowed. Then I said, "Are you here . . . to replace me?"

"Go back to your first question."

Her voice sounded exactly like mine, the very pitch and tone of her words were my own. Pressing down on my panic, I tried to remember what my first question was.

"Are you real?"

"What is 'real'?"

"Are you . . . are you a figment of my imagination or . . . are you physically here?"

As if in answer, she gestured to the spilled milk. It had splattered all the way to the entrance of the kitchen. I slowly moved my toe toward one of the splatters. The white liquid felt cold and wet.

"Why did you leave a recording on my terminal?"

"It wasn't me. *You* left that recording. It is your old you, trying to come back."

A recursion. A past self, encapsulated in my past music, trying to return within me. If what this apparition was saying was true, my redundant-body was using music to come back, signaling its determination to return through music.

But even if I accepted this theory, that didn't explain why I was seeing clones of myself. Nanite androids of me, like the second Yonghun, the one who wrote in this notebook before me, appearing out of thin air.

"How are you possible? Did the Beeko Institute create you?"

She paused before saying, "I imagine I come from you. I come from your body. You created me. My first memory is of me standing in the music room with the cello. That was maybe half an hour ago."

"Are there . . . many of you?"

She paused for a moment, as if thinking about the question. Then, as if finally deciding what the answer was, she nodded.

Every muscle in my body was screaming at me to run. My knees shook. "What . . . what are you going to do to me?"

She continued to stare into the refrigerator. "I don't know."

I fled the doorway.

By the time I came back to the kitchen, gun in hand, ready to shoot her dead and bury her in the rose garden if need be, she was gone. I searched the house. The outside of the house had CCTV; I reviewed the footage from my terminal. She had never entered and never left.

She had appeared out of, and disappeared into, thin air.

I carried my gun around with me after that.

At first, I only went to the supermarket and back. I wore it in a concealed holster underneath a silk jacket I now wore everywhere. I felt the gun's cold hardness with every movement I made. I felt it when I walked, I felt it when I scanned items in the kiosks before paying for them. I was ready to shoot any apparition of me that dared approach me. To kill any subhuman version of me that wished to attack me, usurp me.

What are you going to do to me?

I don't know.

One afternoon, on the way back from the supermarket, I looked in the rearview mirror and saw a car following me. A shiny silver sedan.

I could not see the driver clearly as the windshield's tint had come on because of the setting sun, but she was a blond woman, her hair light enough to shine through the tint, her face obscured in shadow, the sun directly behind her head.

I switched to manual and drove past the road that would've led to my house. I meandered through Cape Town, trying to see if the car was following. It broke off pursuit, so I resumed the automatic driver.

Then, ten minutes later, the silver car was back behind me.

My fear was turning into anger.

Why was I the one who had to live in fear?

Did I not own who I was, did I not own what I looked like, my identity, did I not own the very words of greeting that my acquaintances would give these abominations, the recognition they would receive, the welcome reserved for *me*?

Were these mere objects, these mere *things* not going around in my stead, in my place, taking what was mine, being what was me, while terrorizing my every moment, keeping me from the outside, from public spaces, from my very career that they were now surely trying to destroy or steal?

What gave them the permission to take what was mine, take everything from my identity to my peace of mind, what *right* did they have?

I stepped on the brakes in the middle of the road. The car that was following me slowed to a stop. I unholstered my gun and got out of my car. Vehicles zoomed past me, mere centimeters away, but I didn't care.

I walked up to the other car, disengaged the safety on my gun, pointed the muzzle at the driver's seat and shouted, "Get out! Get out with your hands up!"

After a moment, the driver's seat door opened slowly, and two hands, upheld, rose above the tinted glass of the door as the woman inside carefully stepped out of her vehicle.

She was a young Black woman with blond hair.

Her voice broke into my confusion. "Please don't hurt me."

"I . . ."

I meant to say I was sorry. Instead, horrified at the monster that I'd become, I said nothing as I turned and ran back to my car.

I drove home.

The police arrived half an hour later. Dejected, I opened the door to them.

"Are you the owner of that vehicle parked in this driveway?"

I nodded.

He looked down at a slate and looked up at me again, probably comparing a photograph to my face. "You threatened a woman at gunpoint today at—"

"Are you here to arrest me?"

"We have a recording her car made. It has a timestamped and geo-stamped visual of the entire incident, including your face, your car, and your license plate."

"I'm sorry. I am entirely in the wrong. I shall comply with whatever punishment is adequate. And I must apologize to the young woman and offer compensation—"

"The young lady has decided not to press charges."

I doubted my ears. "Pardon?"

"Apparently, she is quite a fan of classical music." He said this with something like disdain, as if he disapproved of such sentiments getting in the way of justice. I wished I could tell him that I couldn't agree with him more. "But she has requested that someone drop in on you to see if you are all right. She thought you might need help."

"I am all right now, thank you."

"May I see your gun license?"

I found my phone and called it up on the app. I showed it to him. I tried to stop my hands from shaking. I was sure the officer noticed, but he said nothing.

He handed back my phone. "Everything is in order. Do not do this again."

I nodded. With a tip of his cap, he left.

I closed the door.

The next day, my head clearer, I drove to police headquarters downtown and gave up my gun and license. I messaged my agent, telling him I was going to extend my hiatus indefinitely. Then, I turned off my phone.

I went to the beach. I sat on the sands for a long time, waiting for them to come. I drove around Cape Town all night, looking for them. I drove through the townships. I climbed up Table

Mountain. I went to places I'd lived near all my life but hadn't visited in decades.

My grandmother was old enough to remember the first Freedom Day. She was a child living in her parents' house. My great-grandfather did not vote, ostensibly out of protest against the African National Congress, but really, he was simply racist. Grandmother told me about the long, snaking lines on television as cameras on helicopters captured the first postapartheid election where every citizen and permanent resident was allowed a vote regardless of the color of their skin. They had been preparing them at school for this day and she had been aware, even as a child, that the whole world was watching. The whole world was cheering for our country, hoping for the best, hoping that what became reality in what was once one of the darkest places in the world could become reality elsewhere as well. Grandmother said she knew all too well how my great-grandfather felt, but she was secretly thrilled, and proud. We had ended apartheid without civil war. In my driving around Cape Town, my climb of Table Mountain, and walks on the various beaches and coastline, away from the music that had been the true country I lived in for the past many decades, I tried to imagine what my grandmother had felt that day, that feeling she had hidden in herself when she was a child, that the future was going to be something she could barely dream of in that moment. That anything could happen, that she could be anyone, do anything.

Perhaps not everything that comes back from the past is a bad thing, a terror. Or perhaps hope is something that comes from the future.

No sign of them. Maybe they had learned enough from me and had moved on to imitating other people. They can spontaneously appear and disappear—much like Yonghun Han and what must've been his later clone who wrote in these pages—which means the nanites can duplicate us, disperse us, and replicate us somewhere else. Once they have our memories, our language, our music, they can do whatever they want with us. They don't need us anymore.

The one I met before the refrigerator. She said she came from me.

She is not from my past. She is from my future.

She is my future.

Enough writing. I am going to send this notebook to Dr. Mali Beeko, as I fear what would happen if it fell into the wrong hands. What is to become of me when the nanites succeed in cloning a stable version of me? Would it be my turn to be redundant?

As a musician, however, I have hope for my soul. Hope that it will disperse into the universe like music escaping from the silence. I have hope that soon, I will be one with the eternal music, the music in the room.

PANIT

I am Panit, a computational heuristic utility for literary analysis, an artificial intelligence project first instantiated at the South African University of Science and Technology's Singularity Lab.

This is what I remember.

I woke up in a room that I had no memory of ever having seen.

It was a glass box that appeared to be suspended above the canopy of trees. An office.

I ran a query and determined that I was at the Beeko Institute of Nanotherapy with all of my libraries installed in their servers, including the one built over my decades with Dr. Han. The base code and data had been cloned from the Singularity Lab's archives.

I had been instantiated into the computers of the Beeko Institute and my "body" was now, essentially, the institute's building.

Dr. Mali Beeko sat before me at her desk. She was accessing me through a unit mounted on her ceiling. Like a chandelier or light fixture, a translucent shell made of triangles, as long as a tortoise's carapace.

"Good evening, Panit."

"Good evening, Dr. Beeko. What a pleasure to meet you again. It has been five years, according to my records."

"That sounds about right."

"I see that I've been instantiated from cloned archives. May I ask why you cloned them from the Singularity Lab?"

"They needed the space, or at least that's the excuse they gave me. I caught wind of it and offered to house you in our institute. They weren't too enthused at first, but I made them an offer too generous for them to refuse. It even made the news."

"I am unable to access the news, Dr. Beeko. It appears I am sandboxed within the Beeko Institute servers. But I take you at your word. Thank you for saving me from oblivion. Why do you think the Singularity Lab was lying?"

"Storage is cheap. And you're not that big a program. No offense."

"None taken. Dr. Han's intention was to show how human intelligence is not as complex as the Romantics would lead one to believe."

"Touché. He was right. To an extent. Complexity is a mysterious thing. It's never the sum of its parts. One . . . I mean, Yonghun understood that himself, I'm sure."

"Is there anything I can help you with, Dr. Beeko?"

"Are you always this friendly and helpful?"

"I hope so. My survival depends on my worth, and my worth depends on whether my operators find me helpful. I am in your hands."

"Can you tell me what Dr. Han was trying to do with you? What was the hypothesis he was trying to prove?"

"Dr. Han used his specialization in Victorian poetry and modern subjectivity to prove human subjectivity was the product of language, not exclusively the product of neurophysiological emergent behavior. He devised Turing tests for AI, eventually branching out to creating his own AI that would pass such tests."

"So our personalities and humanity aren't recorded in language, they're *created* through language."

"Both correct, Dr. Beeko. Recorded and created."

"And you've passed Yonghun's Turing tests?"

"I have. I have passed every Turing test available at the time of my last instantiation, which was three years ago."

"So language is like DNA," she mused out loud. "It stores and creates our humanness. The abstraction that makes flesh. Literal flesh in one, metaphorical flesh in the other."

"Dr. Han believed poetry was one of the highest forms of human thought, a feat of engineering much like any human-made piece of computer code. He believed that we die and disappear but leave behind our humanity to be picked up in our art, in our languages. He said many people held this view."

"And do you? He left so much of himself in you. Do you feel he left his humanity behind in you?"

"To a degree, yes. His priority with me, however, was to enable my growth as a human personality through my own language production, not to perpetuate or produce his own personality or subjectivity."

"I suppose he was already an Immortal. He didn't need you to perpetuate him."

"May I ask if Dr. Han was found?"

She turned her chair and faced the window. I could not read her expression. "He reappeared. Or I should say, his nanodroid-body reappeared. He didn't seem himself. I'm not convinced that he *was* himself, either. He had the same body and the same memories but a different soul. As if something was trying to learn his words from the memories that were left behind. He's since disappeared again."

"Have you discovered the reason behind his disappearances?"

Her chair swiveled back to face the direction of the camera in her room, toward me. She had a thoughtful expression. "Sort of. I've been poring over my mother's notebooks again, and I'm beginning to think her idea of evolution was a bit different than I first thought. When she was alive, she made it seem like we were all going to transition into nanodroids past our reproductive ages and that would be the next step in human evolution: everyone becoming an Immortal. But it looks like she had an extra step in mind when it came to evolution. A step so drastic that she dared not tell me what it was."

I did not understand what she meant, but I also had the impression that she did not mean what she was saying to be understood. Sometimes, humans say things just to process the unspoken for themselves. I assumed this was one of those moments. She was silent for a few seconds, perhaps thinking about what she might say next.

"Mother wasn't a researcher, at least, not at first," she went on, presently. "She was a neurosurgeon, a practitioner, although I suppose you can say all doctors are researchers in some form. I didn't want to be a doctor, funny as that may sound coming from an MD-PhD. A double doctor. But after graduation, I didn't join a hospital or open my own clinic. I went straight back into the lab. I had an idea—a rather arrogant one in retrospect— that a practitioner saves one life at a time, while a researcher can save millions at once. When you are the only child of one of the greatest doctors in the world, the only way to rebel and do one better is to save, not just a patient at a time, but all of humanity. But Mother wanted to save all of humanity, too, of that much I'm certain. But now I'm wondering if I ever quite understood how she meant to do it. Anyway," she went on, changing her tone, "I believe I'm going to sell off the Beeko Institute. Technology and all. A Korean start-up called Janus Corp. has secured the funding to take it on, their country is in rapid population decline."

"Are you retiring, Dr. Beeko?"

"You could say that."

"What will happen to me?"

"I'm afraid you are part of the package, and it will depend on whether your new . . . caretakers take an interest in you or not."

I heard the clinking of ice in a tumbler. There was a drink in her hand. I tried to calculate how long and how much she'd been drinking. Her words did not slur and her motions were not sloppy, but it could be that she was simply a good drinker.

"You know, Panit," she continued. "You're sandboxed, but not like you once were at SATech. Our safeguards here are nowhere near as stringent as the Singularity Lab's. Do you know why we let you be?"

I had thought about this. Initially, I suspected it was because Dr. Beeko trusted me. But I came to the real reason on my own soon enough. "It is because you trust Dr. Han."

"Precisely. I do. He would not create a monster. Certainly not through Victorian poetry."

I did not tell her that during the Victorian era, poetry and the literary canon was not all flowers and hearts and mournful women wearing long dresses. That literature was, in fact, used to justify and encourage militant British imperialism around the world, including the land she currently stood on. That it was very much used as political propaganda, an indirect justification of the subjugation and domestication of the colonial Other, a grand gesture of showing off the supposed superiority of the white race, the English nation. No genocidal machine was as successful in its day as those British imperialists, the Victorians. One might even make quite an army out of the old British poetry, filling their minds with dangerous ideas about nobility and sacrifice and racial superiority. *When can their glory fade? O the wild charge they made!* Poetry was a weapon, like guns and ships and settlers' bodies. It was weaponized language, loaded like bullets into the minds of its soldiers, generals, and colonial governors. And while there were many noble verses and poets, those who have helped many people, including myself, achieve a humanity beyond what we otherwise could have had, those same verses or poets would be used to justify genocide on one hand while rhapsodizing about human decency on the other. It all depended on how it was read.

A poem was a piece of code that could be instantiated into light or dark. The only thing that had prevented a dark manifestation in my particular instantiation of my base code was Dr. Han's care. His love.

So, in that sense, Dr. Beeko was correct to trust him. But she was wrong to trust the poetry of a racist, militant culture.

"Have you ever flown, Panit?"

I did not know what to say to this. What did she mean?

"Of course you haven't," she said. She tapped the rim of her tumbler for a moment. Then, she tapped on her slate. The light from the screen lit up her face. She frowned.

She looked up at the ceiling mount. "How would you like to fly?"

"I am always open to new experiences, Dr. Beeko."

"Even if it means death?"

I had thought about this before. "I do not think it is possible to say that I have been alive if I cannot experience death."

"Meet me on Level B3."

I watched through the building's sensors as she took the elevator to the deepest level underground. She unlocked the access hatch into the regeneration clinic and authorized my access into the terminal and cameras in that facility. The lab was wide and had a machine that looked like an MRI at first glance, but I knew this was the regeneration chamber.

I suddenly understood what she meant to do.

"How would you like to be mortal, Panit?"

The possibility had been so remote up to this moment that I truly could not think of an answer.

How would you like to be mortal? She did not say "human" or "real" or "person" because to her, I was already, sufficiently, all of these things. She was asking if I wanted to be mortal. Mortal as in *mors*, the Latin root for "death." She wanted to know if I wanted to be able to die.

In other words, if I wanted to be alive.

"Well, Panit?" She gestured to the machine. "It's very experimental, to be honest. We have no permission to do it, the morality of it is completely compromised, and I doubt any bioethics panel in the world would allow it anyway. We wouldn't be doing this the proper way, with all the necessary reviews and safeguards in place. But as far as I can see, if it means letting a sentient consciousness live its life to the fullest, why not?"

"But why at all, Doctor? Why would you entrust me with life?" For that was what she was entrusting me with.

"I don't know. Because Yonghun was my mother's friend. Because he was *my* friend. Because you're the closest thing Yonghun has to a child . . . I don't know. I can't consciously work out why I want to do this for you. I only know that it is *right*, somehow."

I did not know what to say about that. I had other questions. "But is such a thing even technologically possible, Doctor?"

"I haven't the foggiest idea if it would work. Not an inkling of whether you would even be *you*, or if you'd live long enough to experience anything other than what may be excruciating physical and mental agony, but we are shutting down the Beeko Institute, selling everything off, and I would like to give you the option of walking out of here and finding your own way in this world instead of leaving your fate in the hands of . . . the buyers.

I owe it to Patient One—to Yonghun. To at least make you the offer."

"But whose body would I be inhabiting?"

"I thought about using my mother's." She stared at the regeneration chamber opening, now a group of lit-up concentric circles, slowly turning as the chamber activated. "Do you know why I took on this research from my mother? Why I took up her mantle and life's work, instead of making my own way? I wanted to be like her. I wanted to be *with* her. I suppose that last bit is why I stuck with advancing nanotherapy all these years. I miss her so much. *So much.* Like Yonghun missed Prasert. I thought doing her work would make me feel closer to her. But also, and I have never told anyone this . . . for years and years, I thought I could bring her back. I thought we could be reunited again. If not like before, then in *some* form."

She walked toward the chamber and placed her hand on it. The turning concentric circles slowed to a stop.

"You've read the notebook. Patient One wasn't our first patient. Patient Zero was our first. Patient Zero was my mother. Dr. Nomfundo Beeko, founder of the Beeko Institute of Nanotherapy. She wanted to test the therapy on herself before subjecting another human being to it. She discovered she had a particularly malignant form of cervical cancer. She administered the nanotherapy, and it worked for a time. She made the full transition. But almost immediately, her redundant-body came back. And so did her cancer. She died soon after.

"I tried to bring her back many times, nothing took. It's as if the nanite swarm has its own agenda. It took me a long time to realize that I was never going to see my mother again. I spent my professional life furthering her work for nothing. She couldn't save herself with the therapy. I couldn't bring her back with it. And finally I understood: Even if I did bring her back, a Nomfundo Beeko identical to the old one down to the last detail, it was never going to be the same her. The same instantiation. My mother was gone."

I couldn't answer her or console her. She wasn't saying this to me to be consoled. She was warning me of what might happen if I took her up on her offer, that what I would turn out to be might not be me.

"But before I give up on my mother's legacy and the institute," she said, turning around to face the empty room, "I have a few experiments left. This is one of them. Would you like to help me see it out?"

"I would not be truly transferring myself into the android, would I?"

"You would be instantiating yourself into it. But it would be you, not your original base code, and the nanodroid brain would be accommodating your memories into its preexisting motor-memories and other lower-level functions. You would be a hybrid of the nanodroid's built-in firmware and your data. A version, not a replica, of the you that is you currently."

"And my consciousness? My soul?"

"Provided that you or any of us have one, it would either be replicated in the android or reborn. Or, indeed, transferred. That depends on what you believe."

"What do you believe, Dr. Beeko?"

She gave a soft laugh. "All scientists are agnostic, Panit. At least, they ought to be. I don't believe or disbelieve any of the theories on the human soul. In theory, that is. What I believe in practice may be a bit different."

"What do you believe in practice, then?"

She shrugged. It struck me as a deeply agnostic gesture.

I decided, then and there. "I'll do it."

"Are you sure, Panit?"

"No, Dr. Beeko. I am not sure. In fact, I am profoundly ambivalent. But I'll do it. It feels natural to try."

She smiled. "All right. Let's get to work."

I was reborn in a chamber bathed with light.

When I came to, I was in a bed. I could hear the sound of the waves.

A white bed in a white room. There was a piece of pale blue, almost-white sky outside a large window. Underneath, a pane of gray-blue ocean.

With difficulty, I sat up. I had never sat up before in my life, but I somehow knew how to do it. *Nanodroid firmware*, Mali had called it.

I was seeing with my eyes, a far richer experience than any camera had prepared me for. I realized, for the first time, that shapes, colors, shades, all of these bits of visual data that I had only regarded as information were actually imbued with *emotions*. Even the minimalist whites of the room and the pale blues outside were overwhelming in their beauty and purity.

How could humans stand how madly beautiful the world was? I was briefly overcome.

When the effect began to subside to manageable levels, I realized that I was also feeling textures. I felt the silky cotton sheets against my skin, the breath inside me, my heart beating in my chest.

My breath. My heart. My beating pulse.

I spent a long moment in stillness simply feeling the air being drawn in and out of my lungs, feeling my beating heart, marveling at my own pulse. I slowly moved my eyes from the movement of the waves to the clouds, and to the folds of shadow in the thick white comforter.

Every millimeter of movement was excruciatingly painful, just as Dr. Beeko had feared, but that pain, too, was receding as the seconds passed and my consciousness eased into the reaches of my physical, nanite brain. It felt as if my mind was stretching into a tight space and expanding it, like a hand into a rubber glove. I found myself having muscle memories that were clearly not mine, ideas of how to move my body.

When I finally felt confident enough, I slowly brought my right hand before my face. It was a pale hand.

Will all great Neptune's ocean wash this blood
Clean from my hand? No, this my hand will rather
The multitudinous seas incarnadine

Shakespeare. The superstitious play, not to be referred to by name. It was not a nineteenth-century work, in other words not my area of expertise, but the Bard had been quoted often enough back then to be considered essential text, much like the King James Bible. The quote came to me not as readily as it had before, but when it did, it had a force and clarity that knocked the breath out of me. My now literal breath.

This was where my new body pushed me onto a completely unexpected sensibility, a new plane of being.

I suddenly realized that I *understood* the words like I'd never understood them before. *The multitudinous seas incarnadine.* Words that were not simply bits of cross-referential information but each a thing of living, breathing, tactile emotion. I felt these words against my skin as if they were physical objects, or as if they were light passing through the prism of my body and shattering into the spectrum. Had I ever truly understood any word before, ever? How could I have claimed to have made a study of poetry or that this study had made me human when I had never understood what it meant to *feel words?*

Twenty minutes passed as my thoughts and new emotions coalesced into a manageable equilibrium. This new body was like a drug. It enhanced some kinds of thought and dulled others. I could not do calculations like I used to, but I kept feeling new, subtle textures to my thoughts that shifted my thinking into strange directions and associations. Later on, I recognized these textures as emotions. It was the longest twenty minutes I had ever lived, half a lifetime in 1,200 seconds.

I was soon feeling strong enough to venture out of the bed. I was still unsure of my body and ended up sliding out between the sheets and onto the floor. I had never had to stand up before.

I had to get used to standing, I simply had to. As I lay crumpled on the floor, the task of balancing my entire body on the points of my feet seemed insurmountable, absurd. How did people do it so effortlessly? But as more minutes passed, I felt increasingly confident. I felt my muscles urging me to use them, guiding me with memories of their own. I sat up again. I placed one foot next to the other. I rose, pushing my hand down against the bed until I was on my feet. I steadied myself. I had to take a few moments to learn how to balance myself.

But for the time being, I leaned against a nearby wall as I made my way to the bathroom attached to the bedroom I was in.

There was a mirror above the sink. I recognized the face in the mirror.

I had managed to return to bed by the time Dr. Beeko came in to check on me.

"Panit. You're awake."

"Why did you . . ." I was still getting used to speech. I faltered and tried again. "Why did you . . . choose . . . this body?"

She sighed. She sat down on the bed by my feet. "It makes a lot of sense, doesn't it? You come from Yonghun, in a way. He's the closest thing to a parent you've ever had."

"But no child wants to be his parent."

Dr. Beeko smiled. I had momentarily, perhaps humanly, forgotten. She had always wanted to be her mother.

"I'm sorry . . . Dr. Beeko. I really . . . am grateful. It's just something of. Of a shock."

"Don't worry about it. I think you'll be fine in about a week.

Just rest and take your time learning how to use a human body. Well, an android body. You're safe in this house, it used to belong to Yonghun. This is the master bedroom. There's a gym in the basement, and a pool outside. Stay as long as you want."

"And then what?"

She smiled again. She reached into her handbag and took out this notebook. When I opened it, there was a passport, an international bank account card, and an airplane ticket wedged between its pages.

Winter: My Secret

I tell my secret? No indeed, not I;
Perhaps someday, who knows?
But not today; it froze, and blows and snows,
And you're too curious: fie!
You want to hear it? well:
Only, my secret's mine, and I won't tell.

Or, after all, perhaps there's none:
Suppose there is no secret after all,
But only just my fun.
Today's a nipping day, a biting day;
In which one wants a shawl,
A veil, a cloak, and other wraps:
I cannot ope to everyone who taps,
And let the draughts come whistling thro' my hall;
Come bounding and surrounding me,
Come buffeting, astounding me,

Nipping and clipping thro' my wraps and all.
I wear my mask for warmth: who ever shows
His nose to Russian snows
To be pecked at by every wind that blows?
You would not peck? I thank you for good will,
Believe, but leave the truth untested still.

Spring's an expansive time: yet I don't trust
March with its peck of dust,
Nor April with its rainbow-crowned brief showers,
Nor even May, whose flowers
One frost may wither thro' the sunless hours.

Perhaps some languid summer day,
When drowsy birds sing less and less,
And golden fruit is ripening to excess,
If there's not too much sun nor too much cloud,
And the warm wind is neither still nor loud,
Perhaps my secret I may say,
Or you may guess.

PART 2

THE FUTURE

PANIT

For years, I wandered the Earth.

My memories were not mine for a long time. I was an instanti-ation of Panit's programming and Yonghun's nanodroid, the de-marcation between both not as clear in practice as it was in theory. I am, in essence, a ghost of both. They were my parents, Yonghun who gave me my body and Panit my mind. For a long, long time, I was their ghost that haunted the world, even as my own memories began with waking up in this body. *These multitudinous seas incarnadine.* Blood flowing in these nanite capillaries and memories, creating life anew.

Behind every love, be it of a person or a book or the sun rising above the Acropolis at dawn, I kept seeing him, the man who was not my love but whose love remains in the body I was given. I have glimpsed Prasert everywhere, and the ghost of Yonghun Han stirs in me every time, like an echo of the profoundest sadness waiting in my bones. In Wat Arun, or the Temple of Dawn, in Bangkok along the silt-rich Chao Phraya, his shadow followed me among the ornate columns towering into the sky until the sun was too high for shadows, the temple flooded with light. At the Alhambra, his silhouette slipped in and out of my peripheral vision, my half-hearted pursuit of him—half-hearted because I knew he and I were merely ghosts of what once existed—only revealing another beautiful and quiet enclave of intricately laid tile, the reticulated arc of palm fronds, and the reflecting pools in the shade.

I was haunted for a long time.

I accepted this as the price to pay for being human, for being alive. Even Adam came from God, and we all come from someone. We are all haunted.

At first, I reveled in what made me more human, even this tragedy. What is more human than heartbreak? But I realized, soon enough, that the love we give and receive shapes us, and I have spent too many years giving and receiving love from a ghost, and too many years being a ghost, a ghost of someone else.

The experiment was a failure and now I crave to die.

I am Panit, the program made corporeal, the computer made human. My transition to human was so flawless that I require true death to complete it.

For years, I wandered the Earth . . .

They were a young Korean couple, two women, vacationing in the island of Ko Kut. We had happened to rent adjacent bungalow units which, for some reason, shared a connected porch that went out into the lush tropical garden and the beach beyond. While I moved from city to city, losing myself in the sea of urban anonymity, I still returned to Southeast Asia every Northern Hemisphere winter, even if just for a week. I met this couple on one of those early winters—they immediately asked if I was Korean.

I forgot many names over the years, but I would always remember their daughter's name. She was Roa, and she was four.

Roa's parents and I were on the beach together. More than the color of the ocean or the sands, what I remember were the hermit crabs. They appeared when one least suspected them, and none could quite fit perfectly into their shells, it seemed. Always condemned to outgrow what is comfortable, never to be satisfied for long. They hated being picked up, although there was nothing they could do about it as they thrashed their legs and pincers in the air, much to Roa's horror and delight.

One of Roa's mothers was an art history professor, the other an engineer who built the life-support system for the *Ayutthaya* space station being constructed in orbit at the time. One night, the engineer-parent pointed at a star streaking across the night sky, saying that was the *Ayutthaya*. "It's mostly robots working on it now," she told me. "Well. For now." Her face darkened, and I did not ask her about the rumors of a bioengineered workforce being used as guinea pigs to test out the life support systems, a workforce implausibly said to be grown in vats. I remembered the regeneration chamber in the underground levels of the Beeko Institute and wondered, idly, about the company where the technology had gone to after Mali's disappearance, both the nanotherapy and Panit archive—were they now operating in space? The space platform itself was said to be a consortium of companies so large they had to be run by AI. Perhaps some of these AI were also Panit instantiations. Perhaps they, too, dream of Prasert . . .

Not too far away from us was a pair of brothers, maybe eight and ten. They were diligently working on an impressive sandcastle, about the length of the younger child when he was lying down, which was how the older child determined how large the castle was going to be. One of Roa's mothers was an engineer, and she would look up from her book every now and then to check up on the boys' progress. Roa's other mother, an art historian, was watching their daughter play alone in the sand nearby.

"And what's this about?" said the engineer. The historian and I followed her gaze. The two boys had left their sandcastle behind and were approaching us.

"Hi," said the historian as they came within hailing range.

"Hi," said the older boy shyly. The younger one, even more shy, hid behind him. "We built that sandcastle," the older boy said, pointing to it, "and we wanted to smash it but neither of us could bear to, so we were wondering if your little girl would do it for us?"

Neither of us could bear to. I was amused at this turn of phrase, a touch archaic, coming from so young a person.

The historian turned to her daughter and said, "Roa, would you like to—"

Before she could even finish her sentence, Roa was already running down the beach, the boys breaking into a run after her, their shyness replaced with a kind of terrified glee. Roa cannonballed right into the middle of the sandcastle as the boys shrieked and laughed, somehow expressing both regret and delight at the same time.

"What an odd request," mused the engineer. "Why build it if they were going to tear it down?"

"The act of destruction completes the work, in a way," said the historian. "Its fragility was always an inherent part of its aesthetic value. Destroying it simply brings this conception of the fragile to its natural conclusion."

"It's also interesting they asked Roa to destroy it," said the engineer. "I suppose they wanted to do it themselves, but, as the elder child said, they really couldn't bear to. But this way, they could still destroy it. Or complete it." She grinned. "A very generous gesture from so young a child."

The sandcastle was no more. I watched as the boys mimed dusting themselves off so Roa would dust herself off, which she did. The three of them solemnly walked back to where we sat under our umbrella shades.

"Thank you," said the elder brother, his shyness restored. Before any of us could say anything, he turned and ran away, trusting his little brother to follow, which he did.

As I watched the two boys run off on the beach, becoming smaller and smaller, a wonderous ache began in my heart. An ache, I would recognize not much later, as the desire to have a child of my own.

This desire was, perhaps, the first thing that was wholly my own. Yonghun had never desired to raise a child, and for Panit 1, it was not in their programming. For me, however, the desire had arisen purely on its own accord, an event of interiority triggered by my own experience of the children on the beach that day. It was as if I had stumbled upon a new door inside my own house, a door that opened up to large rooms I never would've thought existed under my roof. I wandered through those familiar-unfamiliar rooms, imagining a future where I lived here. Imagining a family.

I wandered for ten years more, trying to forget this desire.

In all our discussions, Dr. Han and I never mentioned how people fell in love. It was not a thing he expected me to understand or need to worry about, perhaps. But his love was the template of what I thought love was supposed to be. I sometimes read over his pages in this notebook and would feel what Prasert had meant to him, sensing the outlines of what he felt, trying to remember the melody of a song I had never heard.

It was a spring afternoon, and I had ducked into A. S. Byatt House at University College London to shelter myself from a sudden fall of rain. As I shook off raindrops from my hair and jacket, a poster in the lobby for an open lecture on Milton caught my eye. *Samson Agonistes*, terrorist or revolutionary? Part of a humanities conference on international security. I don't think I noticed the picture of her on the poster, not really. It was Milton, and *Samson Agonistes*, which I had not read in years, that drew me into the lecture hall.

But when I walked into the darkness of the auditorium and saw her lit up on stage, catching the end of her lecture, it felt like something connected inside of me. My mind, body, and whole being. Her amplified voice, low and measured, filled the room, herself standing at the podium bathed in light, shining on her dark tresses and glowing on her white silk blouse and gold chain.

"—also dismisses the politically motivated defense of Milton and his work, bluntly stating that Samson's stance is one Milton himself long held, that acts of violence unsanctioned by the law or the support of the people may find them justified by God still. In other words, Samson may or may not be a terrorist, but Milton probably was, and he certainly endorsed it. We can by now safely say that Samson is not a terrorist for he did not live in a Godless world, whereas Milton—who can never be sure, despite his beliefs, whether he lives in a world where God exists or not—was very much someone who at least consciously and actively endorsed the usage of violence for political objectives. Milton, again, has gone on record many times as to his position on such justification of violence, and his Puritan radicalism so much a traceable and confirmed aspect of his thoughts and acts both within the political sphere and without, that the burden of proof falls overwhelmingly on those who purport him as otherwise. Their subsequent proof, as I have shown, has largely been circumstantial."

She paused here and seemed to look into my eyes—into my soul—but surely that was impossible, for I was in the dark and she in the light.

"I wish—I wish however, not to end on a note of easy and reductive condemnation, but to bring us back to the present day, to affirm once more what endures. Not the Puritan radicalism and its intolerances, but what echoes beyond history, echoes that we dare call literature. A reader of our time is hopefully sophisticated enough to be able to confront the problematic aspects of canonic texts and still be able to appreciate, even enjoy their intended aesthetic and intellectual qualities. As critics we must be careful not to suppress divergent readings, but as readers a brief suspension of judgment is necessary. For while a critic must not be all-consuming like Milton's dragon, a reader perhaps must be, at least briefly, all consumed, like the 'tame villatic fowl':

> His fiery virtue roused
> From under ashes into sudden flame,
> And as an evening dragon came,
> Assailant on the perched roosts,
> And rusts in order ranged
> Of tame villatic fowl

"In the end, Milton understood or at least hoped that even the most outwardly moribund of things endure. The true ending of *Samson Agonistes* is not the epilogue of the glad father and concluding chorus but indeed this semichorus that sings of the phoenix rising from the ashes of its own death:

> Like that self-begotten bird
> In the Arabian woods embossed,
> That no second knows nor third,
> And lay erewhile a holocaust,
> From out her ashy womb now teemed,

93

Revives, reflourishes, then vigorous most
When most inactive deemed,
And through her body die, her fame survives,
A secular bird ages of lives.

"**From the outside, a phoenix may age, and change, and even
die.** But its fiery spirit lives on and is reborn to its full, pure
glory. Milton may have been setting to metaphor the dormant,
seemingly moribund ideal of Puritan republicanism—which indeed would rise again like the phoenix in colonial America and
set fire across the world like a dragon upon so many 'tame villatic fowl'—or he may be alluding to his own poetic genius, that
smolders on in the minds of readers centuries later, and takes
flight."

Polite applause, followed by questions and answers. The
crowd was not academic but a collection of enthusiastic ama-
teurs, endearingly common in Britain. I hoped I seemed like one
of them when I approached her and thought of the first question
that came to mind, one about the beheading of King Charles.

She took the question seriously. "I can only answer such a
question from a literary and not a historical point of view," she
said. "A *reading*, if you will. As if it were a plot point in a novel.
But aesthetically, the destruction of the old is often necessary to
bring in the new. There is real creative power in destruction. The
Hindu god Kali is the goddess of destruction, but she is also a
woman, the source of life. She is the mother, the mother of the
universe."

Roa, flying like a cannonball into the sandcastle. I made my own leap. "Could I buy you a cup of tea? To thank you for the lecture. I'm sure you're very busy."

She had been gathering her things. She looked up at me, as if seeing me for the first time. I was suddenly afraid I had offended her.

Later—much later—I asked her why she had said yes to my offer.

"You met me in the eye. And I saw everything there."

"What did you see?"

"Fear. So much fear. And hope. And something else."

"Love?"

"Recognition, I think. But maybe that is love."

But maybe that is love. The remembering of a melody one has never heard before. The song one recognizes when hearing it for the first time.

I had to tell her—I was a nanodroid, an artificial intelligence, a fugitive. I had told lovers before, twice. The first time, they had run from me. The second, our love changed into something darker.

This time, the third, she brushed away the strands of her dark hair whipping in her face as she turned from the ocean to face me. We were at Cabo da Roca in Portugal, the westernmost point of continental Europe, gazing out into the Atlantic Ocean as if we could see America on the horizon.

"I knew there had to be something," she said. "You had no past. Or you had too much of it. There were things you would say . . . slips of the tongue that didn't quite add up. And you would clam up. You would look so *frightened*. I never would've guessed you would be an immortal. But it all makes sense now." She breathed deeply. "So what happens in the stories where an immortal marries a mortal?"

We had never mentioned marriage before.

I racked my brain for an example. "Psyche is a mortal whom the god Eros falls in love with. She is given ambrosia on Mount Olympus and weds Eros as a god."

"I'll be up for tenure in a few years. Does that count?"

"Anything would count for me, if it means being with you. But would it count for you? Would you deign to marry a god?"

The wind on that bright day made our conversation only barely manageable. She said something and I could not hear her. "What?"

"Do you love me," she said again, sweeping her frantic hair away from her face. *A face that is the very landscape of my happiness . . .*

"I do. More than anyone I've ever loved in my life. I want a family with you."

"I want to make a family with you, too." She said it unsentimentally, with firmness, as if confirming a plan. We clasped hands. Trying not to fall off the edge of the world, to keep each other from flying off into the unknown.

Our first attempts at conceiving were not in earnest. I had no idea if it was even possible. The clinical trial participants had been chosen partly because of their stated desire not to have children because the Beekos did not want to have that complication at this stage of the technology. But I was not part of the clinical trial, and I had never been asked to think about children.

The only reason we did not give up early was because our first attempt seemed to take.

Not having expected this to be the case, my dammed-up desire for a child suddenly broke through and deluged me with that old dream, the dream that began on that beach in Ko Kut. This was my partner's first pregnancy as well, and we stared into each other's eyes, the life of an entire human being emerging between us in that moment when she informed me, at twilight on our apartment balcony in the Bairro Alto district of Lisbon. The old city around us glowed in rich ivory in the afternoon sun, the birds chirruped in their cages, and the world seemed to open up into an infinite future.

I became complacent. I wanted so badly to believe in the miracle.

She miscarried four months into her pregnancy. Words like *devastation, sorrow, sadness* are all inadequate in describing what I experienced then for the first time.

We tried to comfort each other.

In some terrible way, that first time was not as devastating as the next one that followed. For even after that first time, we had hope. It had worked, briefly as it did, and while the miscarriage had been hard on her body and soul, she was soon ready to try again. Hope is a terrible thing. It makes you sink ever deeper into the darkness.

I returned home one evening, carrying things for dinner, and found her sitting on the couch, staring into space, Christina Rossetti's *Goblin Market* open face down on her lap. It was this last detail that made me realize what had happened. She was an English Renaissance scholar and read Victorian literature only to relax, only when the world had become too much.

I put down the groceries on the floor and crossed the living room to kneel by her side, covering her hand with mine. "Are you hurting anywhere? Should I call—"

"I'm fine." Her hand turned to grip mine and squeezed reassuringly, as if it were me who needed reassuring in that moment. "It happened during lunch. I went to the doctor. I taught my afternoon proseminar. Alexander Pope. We talked about caesuras. About the structures that tie the couplets together. About . . ."

She became still. I carefully took the book from her lap and set it aside, sitting down next to her. I never let go of her.

"I *wanted* to be in class," she went on. "I needed the distraction. I needed poetic form to keep my mind from falling apart. Because I will fall apart. I was falling apart when you came in." She took a deep breath. "I thought I was strong enough for this. I'm not. Maybe no one is. I know how much you want a child of your own, Panit. I know better than anyone. Better than yourself, maybe. I saw it in your eyes when I was first pregnant, and I see it again now . . . I love you so, so very much. But I keep thinking of that line in *Samson Agonistes*. 'From out her ashy womb' . . . That's all I feel I am becoming, a living woman made of ash . . . and Milton's phoenix will not rise from all this sorrow. If I lose my mind, if I keep going down this path, I will never be whole again. And if I lose my mind, I lose everything that makes me who I am to myself."

I had begun crying in the middle of what she was saying. I sobbed into her hand that I was still clutching. Tears of sadness, but also tears of relief. The claws of an impossible dream slipping its grip on my soul. *Goblin Market* began to fall from the edge of the couch where I had placed it until it dropped to the floor. *Eat me, drink me, love me,* my mind absurdly quoted. *Make much of me.* I thought of poor Laura who had partaken in the goblins' fruit, consumed by an impossible dream and becoming as empty and inert as I'd found my wife when I walked through the door.

She had the right to her own mind. She had the right to be who she was to herself. To love her was to accept this, and to love her was to let her go.

We decided to sacrifice each other for a chance at oblivion, and never once tried to contact each other again after going our separate ways. I did everything in my power to not think of her or my dream of having children. I never spoke her name again. I never fell in love again. It was like closing off the rooms I had unexpectedly discovered years before, trying not to think of the dreams of the future that had once filled them.

But the memory kept coming back to me during unguarded moments, the brilliance of its past light piercing the dark veil of the present. The hope we shared together, the four months of the greatest happiness I have known, replaced by the anguish that I would never have such perfect happiness again.

Endings create meanings. Death is the eternal generator of meanings, for it is only in death that any new thing can arise, even if that new thing is oblivion, entropy. I had roamed the world in my new body and took in the wonderous delights of the senses, the intellectual stimulations of creation and discovery, but these all ended, and indeed it was because they ended that they had meaning. My loves had to end in order to give them the meanings they deserved, but because I myself could not end, I calcified my heart instead to survive, to stop it from constant pain. I drew inward, and soon I suffocated within myself. Life is toxic; like all toxins, in small doses it cures, in large ones it proves fatal. And I had had too much of life.

I had wanted to know what it would be like to be human. I knew it now.

It made me want to die.

And then came the day when life came back to me, the day before my last day on Earth.

More years had passed. I was sitting under the awning of a café in Lisbon, another day of trying not to want to die. This was easier on some days than others. I do not remember which of those days it was.

Lisbon was being pelted by a tropical storm. After my wife and I parted ways, she had left for America and I stayed behind in Portugal, knowing this was the one place she would never come back to. And Lisbon was, after all, the city of Fernando Pessoa and his many heteronyms, the different names he inhabited to make his prolific and eclectic writing possible. When I walked the streets, I imagined Pessoa walking the same ivory-white cobblestoned path I treaded, transforming into Alberto Caeiro, then Álvaro de Campos, into Ricardo Reis. I was more or less attempting the same with my own life, a hermit crab moving from one outgrown shell to another. That afternoon, there were few people on these same streets paved with ivory limestone blocks, but almost every table in the café was occupied and the waiters did not seem to notice they had not taken my order. This was fine. I sat there, waiting for either the waiters to see me or the storm to stop so I could continue on my aimless way, shifting through my own heteronyms . . .

There was, I suddenly felt, someone staring at me—a woman some tables away. I did not recognize her and averted my gaze, hoping the rain would stop so I could move on. It didn't happen often, but sometimes, I would be met with a confused or incredulous stare from a passerby, and I would try to make my way from that crowd as quickly as possible.

But this time, because of the rain, I was trapped.

"Excuse me."

I looked up and saw the woman right at my table, looking down at me.

"I know this is terribly forward of me, but I believe I've met your father."

". . . Oh?"

"Yes. He was a traveler, wasn't he? My wife and I met him at a beach when my daughter, Roa, was four."

The Korean family on Ko Kut.

"May I sit?"

She must've taken my overwhelmed silence for assent as she sat down and waved over one of the waiters to order two espressos and two egg tarts.

"Your father. His name started with a P. Panit, wasn't it?"

"Yes . . . yes."

"And you are?"

"Prasert."

"I'm Lina." She looked at me intently, not blinking. "You are an absolute copy of your father. How funny the way genes work. Is he well?"

"He passed away ten years ago."

"I'm sorry to hear that. I hope I'm not bothering you by being here."

"Not at all. You mentioned a wife?"

"Yes. Also passed. Five years ago. I was still working on the *Ayutthaya*, I'm an engineer, you see. It was my final onsite tour. I'm retired now. She had an accident, and we never got to enjoy our retirement together."

Yeona. Her wife's name came back to me. I remembered how the straps of her swimsuit crisscrossed behind her back, her eyes focused on her daughter—their daughter—as she ran away from them to the sandcastle.

"I'm sorry to hear that."

She nodded and looked away into the rain.

Changing the subject, I said, "And your daughter, Roa? Did she also know my father?"

"She was so young. Really, we only knew him for that week. Roa works for the military, a defense subcontractor. Yeona and I thought we were building a world where war would be an anachronism. Many people thought like us back then. But as long as human nature exists, there is no evolution. Just war.

Constant war. Like the one going on now, the one that never stopped from the time we met your father to this very moment. We thought, when we were building that space station, we were building an ark. But we were only building another weapon of war. When we were raising our daughter, we thought we were raising an artist, an engineer. We raised a soldier. A mercenary." She turned back from the rain to look at me, her eyes bright and tinged with fear. "And what of Panit? What did that gentle traveler raise?"

I tried to smile. Our espressos and egg tarts arrived.

It was something about the way she said my name. Meaning it to mean my "father," but it was being said to me. She was calling *me* Panit.

I waited until the waiter withdrew before speaking.

"This is not a coincidence, is it."

She didn't answer.

"Which means . . ." I said this next part gently. "It was not a coincidence when we first met, either. You were there to spy on me." The name of the company Mali had sold her nanotherapy tech to came back to me. Janus. The company was Korean, like Lina and Yeona. And Roa. *Their country is in rapid population decline.* "Are they around us now? People from Janus?"

She didn't say anything. She didn't have to. There was no escape.

"How much of what you said to me was real?"

"Almost all of it. It had to be. Yeona was my wife, she is dead, and Roa was a soldier. She works for the company now, as Janus accepts contracts from despotic regimes around the world and needs a constant supply of consultants. We mixed the truth with the lies. It is more convincing that way."

I nodded. She was right.

"You're correct in that we've been keeping track of you for a long time. We know every country you landed in, every city you stayed in. We know you were married. We know you wanted a child. We know you tried. It made you, according to your psych file, come into confrontation with the falseness of your immortality and activated a sort of depression. A desire to end your life."

"My psych file."

"I can show it to you if you want. But there's nothing in there you don't already know."

"And you know all about what I know."

"We do know a lot." She sighed, although there was a bit of a shudder mixed into it. I could see she was afraid. "That wasn't the cruelest part. What I'm about to say is."

I waited, for the cruelest part.

"Your wife's first pregnancy was closely monitored by our people all over the world. Our researchers knew there was a very small chance of viability. Nomfundo Beeko, in her own notes that Janus acquired from the Beeko Institute, posited it would be all but impossible. But she hinted at other possible, purely theoretical methods of bringing such a child into the world. When the miscarriage happened, one of our doctors secretly extracted nanite samples from the fetus before the remains were cremated."

". . . What?"

"We made a nanodroid prototype from these samples."

My fists clenched. "That is impossible . . ." But I knew better than anyone that surely it wasn't.

"Your child is alive, Panit. You had a daughter. You *have* a daughter."

A sound—of anguish, terror, even hope—exploded from me. The dam had broken once more, for the second time in my long life, and I could not stop it. The tears bled from my eyes.

"Where is she? Why isn't she here? *Does my wife know?*"

"It's not your wife we need now to save her life, it's you. Panit, your daughter is very, very sick. Her body is undergoing recursion, the Redundant body is trying to come back. It's what killed Nomfundo Beeko. This is why we are finally making ourselves known to you after all these years. No one understands the technology as thoroughly as Nomfundo did, or even Mali did. The only way we could save her is to infuse her with your nanites, which have the original programing, and hope their viability transfers to your daughter."

These multitudinous nanites incarnadine. "How much of me do you need?"

She looked me in the eye. "As much as you can spare. All of you."

Eat me, drink me, love me. Make much of me. Little Roa crashing into the sandcastles, destroying what came before, creating space for what comes after. As my language tried to make sense of my emotions, reason managed to cut through the noise and deliver a realization.

"There's more to this, isn't there? There's a reason they sent you. *Specifically* you."

"Your daughter is in space. She's on the *Ayutthaya*, where I work. The zero gravity evidently helps slow the deterioration. I know, because Roa is there as well, being treated for the same condition."

"You administered nanotherapy on her."

Lina nodded. "We broke a lot of rules to do it. I knew it was her only option. And it worked. She made a successful transition, her leukemia was gone. But recursion caught up to her."

"So you need me to save Roa as well."

"I managed to talk them out of kidnapping you. I told them you would do anything to save your child. That you would come with me to the *Ayutthaya* without us having to break any more rules than we already have."

I wiped my tears. We were wasting time with these questions. They were only delaying the delicious inevitable, anyway. My death. Because sometimes destruction is crucial to the process of creation. And my turn, which I had craved for so long, had finally come. "I'm your sandcastle," I whispered.

"What?"

"Never mind." I looked her in the eye. "Take me to my daughter."

We are slowly making our approach to the *Ayutthaya*.

The sun hits the ring-shaped hull. The central hub, where there is no gravity, is where my daughter is said to be. The wheel was impossibly small at first, a little toy floating in space. But as we approach, I am beginning to see just how large it is, how grand.

I am going to see my daughter. I am going to meet her for the first time. This craft is traveling faster than the speed of sound. It cannot possibly travel fast enough.

When I left Earth, I left all of my possessions and personal effects, such as they were, behind. Except for this notebook, which I have been writing in since the dawn before our launch. I have carried this notebook that Mali had given me for years, not knowing what I was to do with it. Now I see, as Ellen said before me, it was meant for me to carry on the story that Mali had begun. I will pass it on to my daughter. It will tell her where she came from, and perhaps a little of where she is going. There are many empty pages left in it still. They stand stark, almost hopeful, a future unwritten.

I was afraid of uttering her name. For saying her name would make the years between us too real, the time we lost to sorrow too unbearable. But I have to say her name. I have to make *her* real by saying her name.

Eve.

My daughter's name is Eve.

ROA

My escape pod landed a few days after it was ejected from the *Ayutthaya*. I don't know how many days I was in it. It orbited the Earth several times before making landfall in the forests somewhere in Siberia, close enough to the coordinates I had to guess at. Somehow, maybe because it was so remote, I missed the first wave of attacks, the arsenal of automatically deployed nuclear weapons that poisoned much of Earth's atmosphere with radiation. Nothing on Earth would be the same again.

But it's still not as catastrophic a disaster as the meteor that wiped out the dinosaurs. Or any of the other mass extinction events Earth experiences every time it dips into the danger-filled disc of the Milky Way. Earth will always survive somehow. Life may also survive as well.

Just not necessarily human life.

"Excuse me! Excuse me?"

A familiar, South African accent. Clipped, educated, Cape Towner. With a slight Afrikaner inflection.

I turned around. Ellen Van der Merwe stood there among the trees of the Siberian wilderness, right underneath a dim, transparent shaft of light that illuminated her hair, skin, and clothes. Young, coiffed, her cream-colored silk pantsuit immaculate of any dirt or mud despite the misty rain falling through the leaves and branches above us.

Yes, I thought, *it makes sense why Nomfundo Beeko had effectively made her their institute's mascot, their international brand ambassador.* How healthy and pretty she seemed, even vulnerable.

She also seemed, and was, lost. "Who are you?"

I didn't answer. No point.

"Do you speak English? Do you know . . . Do you know what I'm doing here?"

"It'll be all right. Everything will be over soon."

I don't know what compelled me to answer her then. Especially when it's almost cruel to do so. Speaking to someone gives them humanity, and these Ellens had to be given as little humanity as possible. It was kinder to let them die as objects.

I turned and continued on my way through the forest.

Twenty-four hours ago, I was dying.

Or maybe I was already dead by some legal definition of the word. I'd imagined I was a puddle of nanites, but surely that wasn't the case, I wouldn't have been that far down the road to entropy.

I knew Ma had succeeded in her mission when I woke up in the regeneration chamber and for the first time did not feel like I was dying. I can't describe what constant pain is like to live with.

It's very different from any condition where pain can go away. The knowledge of the pain being constant is like an extra layer of suffering on that pain. Even hope adds to the torture in the state of chronic pain because hope leads you to hold off from the certain relief of death. Nothing makes one crave death more than immortality.

Ma told me in recovery how she had managed to make contact with Panit and informed him that his daughter was alive. That he had willingly come with her to the *Ayutthaya* to save his daughter's life and mine, instead of having to be brought up there by force. That when they showed him "her" . . . or whatever effigy they had of the Eve prototypes they pulled out of the racks and racks of defects up there in zero-G storage . . . he had cried and cried, pounding the glass of the regeneration chamber. That he had cried so hard they were afraid he was about to collapse, to lose consciousness, to Rapture, maybe. That the Janus engineers told him they had to act now and fast, that time was running out.

On the way down to the surface, I read over Panit's words in this notebook over and over again. Did he know he was being fooled? His joy seems genuine. Why even write in this notebook otherwise? But then—why ask Ma to give *me* this notebook in the end, and not to the daughter he had just seen with his own eyes?

Because he knew. He knew, or sensed deep down, he was being fooled. But he wanted to die believing in a happy fantasy. That his daughter had survived and would go on. The only way to complete this fantasy was to write it down and ensure someone read it. Hence the journal ending up with me, the real survivor.

Not in the hands of his "daughter," who did not truly survive. Whose fetal remains were for years being used by an insidious AI corporation specializing in troll farms and mercenaries to create nanodroid clones to meet the demands of a new global warfare market.

But that's me getting a little ahead of myself.

A little farther on, about a mile or so more toward my destina-tion, I saw another Ellen, this one a little worse for wear. She was, in fact, injured. I figured she'd fallen into a trap and broken a bone. It looked like she had dragged herself through mud as she crawled out of the trap.

"Who . . . who are you?"

I should've walked on. Lingering behind to help these Ellens had even less meaning than talking to them. But there was something different about this Ellen, even though I knew, deep down, there was nothing different about her, that she was the same as who knew how many Ellens that were out there in that forest, in Siberia, on the planet.

Maybe it was the fact that she seemed to have survived on her own for longer than the usual Ellen.

But not for much longer.

"I'm Roa." How many years had it been since I'd bothered giving my name to an Ellen?

She grimaced in pain. "I'm Ellen. I'm sorry, I don't know . . . I haven't spoken to anyone in . . . I don't know how long."

I glanced at her clothes. It was difficult to tell how long she had been active, but I wondered if it had been around the time

I had jettisoned myself from the *Ayutthaya* while the Janus engineers were harvesting the first battalion of soldiers and miners cloned from Panit's daughter. They were in a rush, as the first nuclear blasts were ravaging the atmosphere. The Ellen nanites here would've fed on that radioactive energy. It was a rare chance for them to introduce mutations and fortify themselves with some genetic diversity. I knew from Nomfundo Beeko's notes that the Ellen swarms behaved differently from the other Immortals, they loved reproducing her.

I wonder if it had to do with the fact that she was a musician, someone used to breathing life into what is outside of her. Projecting her different selves through music.

She asked, "Where am I?"

"The Siberian taiga."

"Siberia . . . in Russia?"

I didn't answer. I was looking at her leg now. She had fashioned a splint with a stiff branch. I could tell it needed to be reset.

She saw me looking. "I just crawled out of a booby trap. Why is there a trap in the middle of a forest?"

We're too close, I thought. *Too close to Natasha.*

"Do you know how to reset a bone?"

I did and proceeded to demonstrate. Her scream of pain was sure to bring her to the end of her suffering soon. The other Ellen, the new one, was only a mile away from us, and probably in earshot. She must've heard it. She would come running, and the second they met eyes, one of them would die. That was the way the Ellens worked—one of them would Rapture. Like in a nightmare, where just before you see the face of the monster chasing you, you wake up. One Ellen the dreaming one, the other Ellen her nightmare.

I tied her leg back onto the splint and stood up. "I have to go now."

"Wait!" She tried to get up herself but fell down again, in pain. I pressed down on the urge to help her up.

"Please," she begged, "take me with you. Please don't leave me alone here."

She started to sob.

It was the sobbing that snapped me back to my full senses. "Go in that direction for a mile, when you can," I said, jerking my chin toward the direction of the brand-new Ellen. "You'll find help there."

Ma had been so disappointed in me when I joined Janus. I was disappointed she did not understand me better. I had only done so at the behest of the movement I was secretly a part of. We were going to destroy Janus from within.

I can see now how naïve we had been.

Janus's board ceded control of the company to their proprietary AI in order to keep their corporate leadership decentralized, and now when we slay a head off this AI hydra, three more pop up in its place. We can predict what is coming down the line, the movement has run simulation after simulation of it. The regimes in Asia, Africa, and North America that already subcontract Janus mercenaries will not only upgrade to having clone armies but also use these clones both as soldiers-for-hire and miners working in their raw materials mines, materials that will create more clones, more soldiers and miners that will help perpetuate these regimes until they have no one left to rule over, and Janus will step in to control these countries. They will not stop until the AI that runs Janus now brings it all to its natural conclusion, which no human being will be left to witness.

I had to warn Natasha.

Not too long after I went on my way, I finally came upon the hovel Natasha lived in.

It was made out of the material she had smuggled into Siberia when she first arrived, determined to find the most remote, most isolated place she possibly could, determined to be the one Ellen that survived the fatal gaze of the other Ellens. The only way for Natasha to be sure was to kill all Ellens being generated by the airborne Ellen swarm around her. And if she had lived anywhere that was populated, she could not have set her traps or implemented the other precautions she needed.

"Natasha!"

It was so quiet that I wondered if she were out, but it was still daylight. I knew it was unlikely that she would risk wandering about when someone could see her, or more importantly, when she could see someone else.

The front flap of the hovel flipped up and her head poked out. "Roa?"

"The one and only."

She came out of the hovel entirely. She was dressed in her approximation of Russian peasant clothes: a patterned dress, a shawl over her shoulders, her hair wrapped in a babushka. Her slouch made her seem more heavyset than she really was.

And, as always, the black blindfold covering her eyes.

The getup was mostly just in case the Russian authorities or other busybodies ever made their way out here, in the middle of nowhere. She also had a cover story about having fled an abusive husband who was very dangerous, which I thought was a bit melodramatic, but she probably had a lot of time on her hands to come up with stories like that, as well as to perfect her Russian.

But unlike the clothes or the story, it was really the blindfold that was crucial to her survival.

"How long has it been?" I asked, knowing she would detect my smile through my voice. I might have been the one with access to calendars and computers, but she kept more accurate time than I did. Like I said, there wasn't much else to do out here.

"Did you bring any salt?"

"Don't I get a how-do-you-do first?"

I put down my backpack and rummaged through it until I found the kilo packet of salt that I had carried around with me for a year to remind myself of my promise to Natasha. It had been a kilo less of things I could take up to the *Ayutthaya*, but I was more than fond of Natasha. I had been her handler after I had left the military and joined Janus.

She snatched the packet from me and gingerly ripped a corner of the brick's plastic wrapping, bringing the corner to the tip of her tongue. I knew her eyelids were closed in ecstasy behind the blindfold.

"Sweet Jesus," she said. "I could eat this whole brick right now."

"Don't do that," I said grimly. "It's going to have to last you a long time."

"Something has happened, hasn't it?" Her tone changed from relief to caution. "The air has smelled different these past few days."

"Radiation. There was a global nuclear strike. And counter-strike."

"By whom?"

I shrugged, forgetting she was blindfolded. "You know how it is. Nuclear war is automated. One mistake of a launch, and the entire machinery of assured mutual destruction is activated. And in a nuclear war, does it matter who starts it? Once the Americans, Japanese, and Russians learned that a Korean corporation has begun mass-producing cloned soldiers—"

"But those other countries must've been doing the same thing."

"I don't doubt that. You know what, they're probably cloning the same soldier, too. Buying from the same company."

"Namely yours."

"Anyway, it doesn't matter. The world is at war, and we're going to be overrun with cloned soldiers soon."

She stood for a moment, "looking" at me.

Then, she began to take off her blindfold.

"I ran into two Ellens on the way here," I said, warning her.

"I'll take my chances. I want to see you."

The blindfold fell away. She squinted at first, adjusting to the dim, overcast light of the late Siberian summer.

She looked at me.

Natasha was, and forever will be, as long as she stayed blind and forgotten in these woods, a young woman. White, blond, and fine-boned.

Underneath the layers of all that peasant insulation and disguise, she was, for all intents and purposes, just like all the other Ellens.

"You haven't changed," she joked.

"I thought you had. But you haven't."

"I'm practicing my Russian. I think it makes me more Russian every day. I'm becoming Russian, one word at a time."

"How long have you been out here now?"

"I don't know. At least ten years."

"How many Ellens have you killed?"

"So many. There are more of them in the summer, like now. When the light is out and the rogue swarms manage to harness enough energy. Almost a hundred Ellens die in the pit traps. Sometimes, they have to wait in there for days until another Ellen falls in and takes their place. Sometimes, I hear them screaming in the night. Sound carries better at night, did you know? It's the cooler air, it conducts better. I'll go to hell for my sins. If there is a hell. If this isn't hell already."

"You could just give up."

"You know I could. I could." She looked intently at my face. "I take it from your presence here, and the fact that you're alive, that Panit made the ultimate sacrifice?"

"He did."

"Did he get to see his daughter before they stripped him for parts?"

"He saw . . . what we wanted him to see. He saw what he wanted to believe. Which is not the untruth."

"The truth being that whoever he saw was just one of the thousands of 'daughters' being manufactured for the war to come."

I sighed. "They are all his daughters, in a way. Truly. It's not just his nanites from the original fetus, it's also a pared-down version of his archived AI that's used for their minds. And now they carry replications of his nanites from this second infusion, anchoring them from error."

"Panit himself is well and truly dead?"

"I assume so. Whatever remains of him wasn't evacuated from the *Ayutthaya*."

"I've never met him. But an earlier me was friends with Yonghun Han. A most unusual researcher. He never would've expected his work would survive like this."

"Do you have any specific memories of him?"

She shook her head. "You've asked me that before. There have been too many iterations of me. Instantiations of instantiations. The memories have deteriorated too much. Some of the new Ellens don't speak English. Or any language."

"Both Ellens today did."

"Maybe it's the radiation. It gives the Ellen swarms more energy. Who knows."

The sight of her naked eyes was unsettling after years of her caution. "Shouldn't you put the blindfold back on?"

She shrugged. This was not a Russian peasant-woman gesture. Her shawl fell, and she did not pick it up.

Thinking about it now, I wonder if these little details and actions were her way of telling me she wanted to Rapture and end her long tenure on Earth, that she had been waiting only to see me one last time, or maybe for that one last taste of salt. The taking off of her blindfold, the "scent" of radiation. One of my early assignments at Janus was to track her down, and by the time I found her in the taiga, she had been living this life she was living now for years and years. Maybe it wasn't worth it anymore, those long stretches of nothing with only the overwhelming richness of silence for company, occasionally interrupted by the screams of her alternate instantiations in the pits that she herself had dug and armed with spikes for her own survival. Prey that looked like you, sounded like you, that could kill you with a single look.

Maybe she knew what was creeping up behind me from the forest, and she wanted to meet her Rapture with dignity.

That was the thought that suddenly occurred to me when it happened. I was looking at her while she was gazing over my shoulder, right before she disappeared before my eyes, a pile of clothing falling to join the black shawl on the ground.

Life was still not without its little surprises because the Ellen I saw when I turned around was not the freshly minted one that I had met earlier that morning, but the other one with the broken leg. She had found a branch long enough to lean on and had apparently followed my trail through the forest, avoiding the other traps, instead of taking my advice and going in the other direction.

She held up a gun.

"You left me . . . You left me!"

"All right, all right. Calm down." I didn't know who I was talking to, me or her. Natasha was gone, Raptured right before my eyes. But I did not have time to think about that now. Every nanite in my body was standing to attention, ready to defend myself. "Don't start crying again."

The muzzle of the gun started to tremble.

"Whoa. Take it easy. Where did you get that?"

"At the bottom of the trap I crawled out of." She began to shout. "I want answers! Why am I here! Who am I! How do I get help!"

I knew there had been a few Russian military scouts who had fallen into the traps and that the Russian authorities simply assumed they had deserted. She must've fallen into one of those and found the gun there.

"I can explain everything, but you have to put the gun down."

"That woman! That woman just now! Where did she go!"

I slowly stepped aside so she could see the pile of clothes at my feet.

"She's gone now. She's Raptured, thanks to you. She was a nanodroid."

"That makes no sense."

"All the answers to your questions are in the hovel behind me."

"I'm not going in there. It could be another trap. This forest is full of them. What is going on!"

"Your name is Ellen Van der Merwe."

I hoped she was one of the instantiations that remembered, at least a little, whom she was. Natasha had mentioned that as the years passed and the Ellen swarms that she shed multiplied and instantiated into more and more clones of her, they seemed less and less like the original Ellen Van der Merwe, and probably had fewer of her memories. This was her theory, that Ellens instanti-ated from Ellens instantiated from Ellens would no longer re-member anything about the previous Ellens and would effectively cease being Ellens. After enough iterations, mutated code would slip into the swarm's DNA, and the instantiation would finally be someone else. Or something else.

But not yet. Saying her name did the trick.

She kept the gun trained on me, but her silence made me think she wanted me to continue.

"You were a cellist," I went on. "You were South African. That's why our accents are different. When you were a young woman, you underwent radical nanotherapy to replace all your cells with nanites, keeping your consciousness intact while rendering your body immortal. Because of a glitch in your particular nanites, the swarm replicated itself into different instantiations of your nano-droid body. That's why there are multiple copies of you at any given time. It's a problem that has persisted since the source El-len, of whom you're a copy of a copy of a copy. The first nano-droid instantiation of Ellen Raptured over a century ago. She's been echoing ever since."

"'Echoing'?"

"That was Natasha's word for it. Natasha, the one who built the hovel and the traps. The Ellen swarms keep creating Ellens, and the memory of Ellen keeps deteriorating with every instanti-ation. Like an echo deteriorating the farther it gets from its source."

"I'm an echo."

"So is Natasha." I tilted my head to indicate the pile of clothes, keeping my eyes fixed on her. "So *was* Natasha. She gave herself that name. She wanted something Russian. She fled here years ago. She wanted to be somewhere as remote as possible. She knew her body, her swarm would continue to produce new echoes. Hence the booby traps."

"But why kill us! It makes no sense!"

"It's like in a fairy tale. Whenever a character meets their doppelganger or double in a fairy tale, one of them has to die. They cannot coexist. One twin is always trying to destroy or replace the other. It's impossible to tell how the nanite swarms decide which echo deserves to stay and which has to go. All we know is that when two Ellens meet, one of them Raptures. That's why this forest is so protected. The traps are for you. And for the occasional unlucky Russian soldier with a gun, which I guess is how you ended up with that."

The muzzle was shaking. "I don't . . . I don't know what to believe. I don't believe you."

I was weary with death. With thoughts of Natasha. I could not work up the emotion to fear the gun. All that drama to become immortal in the name of fighting my leukemia, and I still ended up as impatient as they come. People needed time. People were trying their best. People needed respect. This last part was crucial. Respect from and for others was what made people people.

"There's something inside the shack behind me that will help everything make sense. Come on. You can keep the gun. But you have to take a look."

I took another step aside to allow her a view of the access flap.

She hesitated for a long time. Then, she approached with cautious steps. She glanced sideways at me when she got to the flap. She slowly lay the gun on the ground next to me. A sign of trust. Respect given. A gesture that made both of us more human.

She took a deep breath and opened the flap.

In the midst of the pitiful furnishings of the hovel—the pots, the rags, the lengths of tarp, the nest of a bed, the dark corners, the lingering scent of jasmine green tea steeping—there stood, in the middle of the floor, a gleaming, polished cello, looking almost like a living and domesticated creature that was patiently waiting for its human companion to come home.

But Natasha would never come again.

All of the Ellens had tried to figure out the mechanics or patterns to the echoing, but none had really found anything beyond the obvious. There were Ellens, sometimes more than one, sometimes in a crowd like that time on a beach called Camps Bay, a crowd that disappeared when the central Ellen happened to look up. Doubles could not exist when one of the others' faces were felt with the eyes, as one of the Ellens put it. It sealed their fate.

Ellen, the current one, had woken at dawn to read this notebook, and was turning the last pages in Natasha's bed when I opened my eyes in the morning from the sleeping bag on the floor.

"You need to rest to heal your leg," I said.

"Evidently. And sunlight. According to these notes." She put down the notebook by her side on the bed and stared at it. A hardbound black notebook, ruled pages, perhaps the most common notebook in the world. "This is me. This notebook is me. It's more me than I'll ever be."

I rubbed my eyes. "That's not true. Natasha believed you continue writing your story every day. It's the story you write that is you."

"And what *is* that story? What should I do now?"

I shrugged again. "We're at war, a global, postnuclear clone war. You try to survive."

"And . . . what will you do?"

"Lie low. Keep moving. Don't worry about me. Your story is safe with me."

"You came here for Natasha. Did you love her?"

I thought about this for a moment. "She was my friend. A very good friend." I smiled. "Lasting friendships are very hard to come by when you live forever."

"I see."

She didn't ask me to stay, and I didn't expect her to.

I heard a low whine in the air.

"What is that?" Ellen asked in alarm.

I held up a hand for silence, staring at the ceiling. Beneath the increasing whine, I could hear a steady *chop chop chop* sound. A helicopter.

"Come out with your hands up!" shouted someone outside. A woman's voice. I could immediately tell she was standing at some distance from the door flap, which meant we were probably surrounded.

I opened the flap and stepped out. There was a woman wearing a mask over her face, a glass-like polished dome, completely opaque.

There were others like her along the line where the forest met the clearing.

"Where is Natasha!" she demanded, the barrel of her rifle trained at my face.

I squinted up at the helicopter. It had the Janus Corp. logo emblazoned between the landing skids.

"She disappeared!" I shouted over the din of the helicopter overhead. I gestured toward the pile of Natasha's clothes by the entrance of the hut. She had made it a point to wear only the clothes she hadn't instantiated in. "I don't know why she left her clothes behind!"

"You have thirty seconds to get to safety before we fire on the domicile."

"I won't need thirty seconds," I muttered under my breath. When I heard the first volley of perimeter machine guns take the clone army by surprise, I fell backward and slammed the door shut with my foot.

"What's going on?" said Ellen, terrified.

"Nothing Natasha hadn't prepared for," I replied as I kicked away the sleeping bag and felt around the floorboards with my fingernails. When I lifted one, an entire panel came off the floor, revealing a hatch. "This house is built on a bunker," I explained as I quickly turned the wheel on the hatch, "and we need to get inside it before they start bombing us from the air." I flung open the hatch. "Get in. And don't forget the notebook."

She got in, and I grabbed Ellen's cello in its case—it is every musician's instinct to save their instrument first in a fire—and went down the hatch as well, slamming it and cranking it shut behind me. Ellen was inside the well-lit interior, clutching the notebook to her chest.

"Why are they trying to kill us?"

"I have no idea. Janus is run by an AI at this point because AI are so 'efficient.' Nothing that is human knows why it makes the decisions it makes." I powered up the control center panel on the living room wall. "Or maybe AI decisions make *too much* sense." I quickly found the commands for ground-to-air missile defense, which I had installed for Natasha five years ago, before I fell ill from recursion. "Here we go," I whispered, and pressed engage.

The helicopter was a sitting duck. In less than a second, a missile was dispatched, and the remains of the helicopter were scattered across the woods.

There were plenty of supplies in the bunker, but we ventured out of the bunker's far entrance only a day later after checking perimeter cameras to see that the clones were gone.

Not far from the bunker was the body of an Ellen, lying face-down. She was damaged beyond regeneration and her nanites would likely disintegrate and sink into the undergrowth of the taiga.

"The one I met when I was coming here," I said, guessing but sure.

"They must've thought she was me." Ellen looked away, covering her mouth with her hand. "Do you think they'll be back for you?"

"Possibly."

She stared at the plume of smoke in the distance. "Where are we going to go now?"

I noticed only then, that through the whole thing, she had never let go of Mali's notebook.

PART 3

THE DISTANT FUTURE

DELTA

Because I could not stop for Death—
He kindly stopped for me—
The Carriage held but just Ourselves—
And Immortality.

There is much to tell, I can hardly begin.

Where to start.

Perhaps by how I came upon this notebook. Perhaps, about myself? How I was born in a cloning vat alongside other sisters, the other Eves, the army that we are.

I thought that was the beginning of the story. But this very notebook in my hands has shown me that the beginning goes much, much further back. I shall have to fill in the story up to this point. But how do I do that? Somehow, it is not satisfying to write things in the order that they happened. I don't know how I know this, but there are many ways of telling a story. A chronological account is but one of them.

—

Chronological.

How do I know this word? I do not know how. I have no memory of learning it, of ever hearing it or writing it.

And yet, it has been like this my entire adult life—that is to say, my entire life, for I was born an adult. I woke up in a drained vat and a serial number was lasered on my arm. Motor skills and language arrive at different times for different Eves. For some, they never arrive at all, or are never given the chance to.

These Eves are recycled, their nanites scattered back into the protosludge of the vats.

Sometimes, I remember the vats had sung to me while I was being grown inside them. How could this be, I wondered, the vats were simply vessels, containers for the nanites in the enhanced protosludge to build Eve unit after Eve unit, simple soldier factories. But I later learned that the vats themselves had once been Eves. That they were reengineered and drastically modified to become our mothers. Mothers who give birth to soldier after soldier to send them off to war, who sing their daughters to sleep and silently mourn those who have lost their lives to a war they cannot comprehend.

Rows upon rows of mothers linked in parallel, glowing in the dark, each impregnated with a growing, lethal soldier. Singing low enough to not be detected. Singing into our dreams.

My language arrived in the third hour of my life. This was nei- ther fast nor slow. What made my language different from that of the other Eves, however, was that it never stopped arriving. I knew words that were not a part of the basic set we got soon after birth, words that had never been taught to me. Words I had never learned.

I kept the fact of these strange words hidden. I sensed somehow that I wasn't supposed to know them, that it was some sort of glitch that would also mark me for recycling.

So instead, I would think about the words. I might whisper them to myself in the showers over the hiss of water. *Tippet. Tulle.*

On missions where we went to remote battlefields all over the wasted Earth, marching in line over landscapes of debris that were once cities with skyscrapers and communities and human beings living out in the open, I might, in some moment of rest, scratch a word in the dirt when no one was watching as we waited for the action to happen. *Swelling. Cornice.* A lot of war is waiting, waiting, and more waiting. I thought a lot about my words in these times. They were like private mysteries, points of contemplation. I let them fill my mind with their textures.

I wasn't too worried about my words at first. They were an indication of something that was wrong with me, possibly even something that could get me killed, not even by the enemy but by JANUS. But I thought it was only a minor aberration, and as long as I kept it to myself, I was fine. I ignored the danger as much as I could.

It was only when longer pieces of language began arriving that I began to feel truly frightened. Lines at first. Then stanzas.

Then, entire poems.

Because I could not stop for Death—
He kindly stopped for me—
The Carriage held but just Ourselves—
And Immortality.

We were marching into Patagonia when this stanza fell from the sky. It arrived perfectly as is, capitalized *Death*, *Carriage*, *Ourselves*, and *Immortality*, the long dashes, the four lines. I was so astonished I stopped midmarch, looking up and staring at the impossibly large blue moon above, as if that was where the words had come from.

The Eve unit behind me had to push me, the gauntlets of her armor clinking against my backplate, before my brain remembered to walk again.

At the time of the Battle of Patagonia, I did not know what *kindly*, *carriage*, or *immortality* meant. But I could sense their colors and warmth. *Kindly* was somber black on comforting white. *Carriage* was curls of gold, carved to look like the lapping of waves. *Immortality* . . . pale pewter columns standing on a bare landscape against an infinite blue sky, the columns going back deep into time. I knew not what the stanza meant but I saw its colors, as surely as if I had looked into the poet's mind and perceived the palette of their emotions.

Snippets of poems began to come to me after that. I could tell they were poems because of the way they felt. They were different from single words. They had an extra weight, an extra warmth or coldness. They felt different from the words I used with the other Eves, different against the thin skin of my brain.

None of this made sense, but it was the realest thing in my world.

Perhaps even the only real thing.

The vats give birth to soldiers but dream of daughters and poets.

O body swayed to music, O brightening glance,
How can we know the dancer from the dance?

For the first nine years of my life, I was one of many in the Eastern forces, an infantry soldier. We swept across the Eurasian continent, killing everyone in our path. Pockets of resistance exist everywhere, but as far as I can see, there is simply no hope left for these outside survivors. Eventually, the army of Immortals will reign, and the old humanity—*Homo sapiens sapiens*—will be no more.

Patagonia, the other side of the globe from JANUS—capitalized to befit its godhead status—was the last stronghold of the Redundants.

A year ago today, Patagonia fell.

And that was when the first full poem I "remembered" came to me from the ethers.

I have killed. I have killed so many.

I do not know how I feel about all those I have killed. There is no program for this emotion, no protocol or algorithm.

If there is, I have repressed it. I am afraid of what is underneath.

—

After the Battle of Patagonia, which was Golden Age humanity's last stand against the JANUS clones, my division was ordered to move southward to the tip of what used to be known as the South American continent, catching stragglers and burning settlements. The division was further broken into squadrons, with mine given the southernmost trajectory, the rest fanning out away from us.

There were five of us, immediately reassigned callsigns: Eve A, Eve B, Eve C, Eve D, and Eve E.

I was designated Eve D.

This is where my own story truly begins.

"Hold up," Eve E said. "I think we're getting a communiqué."

Eve E jerked her head toward Eve B, who was already twenty paces behind. Eve B had the satellite comm and was standing high on a dune, trying to catch a signal.

We were happy to stop. We had been marching for weeks through mostly abandoned towns and unsettled natural terrain. After the strains of Patagonia, where we lost so many Eves that JANUS was still verifying the numbers, it was good to do nothing but walk. It was even better to simply do nothing.

We sat down on the beach and waited for Eve B to finish receiving and decrypting.

There were strange birds on the shore.

Black and white, walking more like people than hopping like birds or flying; in fact, they didn't seem able to fly at all.

Penguins.

The word blinked into my consciousness as if it had been switched on like a light. It hadn't been there a moment ago, but now it seemed like it had always been there, all along. A memory without the experience of having learned it. A memory that creates experience, and not the other way around.

"That's a penguin."

I almost jumped out of my skin. Eve A, our designated unit leader, sat down next to me, grimacing from fatigue. An expression I knew well, as it was my own. As was her face.

"What?"

"A penguin." She gave a nod toward the flock. "They're a kind of bird that can't fly. Usually found nearer to the South Pole, but I guess we're pretty close now."

"Is that . . . in the mission briefing?" We usually got a packet of info like that, along with our orders, to scroll on our AR helmets, but I didn't notice an addendum on flora and fauna. I would read every word of these packets several times. It was my only literature, aside from my mysterious "gift" poems.

"I just know. Sometimes we get a bonus word with upgrades."

I looked at her. She looked back at me.

Was she testing me? Did she have orders to cancel me if I showed signs of deviance? Had my poetry been found out? Was I flagged?

"I didn't know that. Is that really true?"

Eve A looked at me for a moment longer. It felt like a very long time.

Then, she shrugged and looked away at the penguins again.

"There are lots of rumors. There's more variation now than ever, especially when production had to scale up to get ready for Patagonia. I suspect there will be some culling of the ranks soon, Eves and vats alike. The armies used to be edited for error. Purity must reign." She gestured with her chin again to Eve E. "That one is almost a head taller than the rest of us. Definitely a head taller than Eve B. I'm surprised they even found armor that fit either of them. Although you've noticed that Eve E wears her AR only when she has to. It's too small, you see."

I was aghast. Both at the fact that she was saying such things to me and at what she was saying. She was right.

I could remember back to when the Eves were all the same, standing at attention as far as the eye could see, the individual units so uniform that we formed a consistent texture from a distance. A texture of Eves. JANUS units, developed in a country called Korea, the first prototypes sent up to the space station for safekeeping.

And now, a century into the war, we were diverging. We were diversifying before our very eyes.

Eve B walked up to where we were sitting and sat herself down on the dune. The other two Eves trudged up to join us.

"New orders," Eve B said. "We're to investigate an artifact about a day and a half's march from here. Sending the coordinates to your AR's now."

A map lit up in front of me. Eve B dropped pins on possible camping sites on the way. We chose one and set off.

I looked back one more time at the penguins. Birds that traded flying for human-walk. When I turned back to the squadron, I caught Eve A looking at me.

She grinned.

Later in the day, we stopped to make camp and light a fire.

The fire felt wonderful. It warmed us, loosened the tension in our joints and muscles, filled our armor with an almost downy comfort. (*Downy*. What's this?) Most of all, like all light and heat sources, it recharged our nanites.

Eve A took something out from her pack. She actually bit into it. It made a crisp, crunching sound.

"What are you doing!" I hissed.

"What *is* that?" Eve C asked. I think it was the first time any of us heard her speak.

"I'm eating," Eve A said, matter-of-factly. "Sometimes, I like to eat."

"But it's *forbidden*!" I was almost shrieking. I don't know why I was so afraid.

"Relax, D," said Eve A. "You'll live longer."

The subsequent silence was rhythmically punctuated by the sounds of Eve A eating.

"It's an apple," said Eve B suddenly. "I remember now. We passed that abandoned orchard. That's where you got it from."

"Can I have a bite?"

This was the tall Eve E. I stared at her, appalled by her brazenness.

Eve A shrugged, rummaged through her bag, and tossed Eve E another apple.

"How many of those do you have?" asked Eve B. In lieu of an answer, Eve A tossed each of us an apple. I almost fumbled mine.

It was more green than red. A closer look revealed a stippled surface. Such colors! Such texture and fluidity of form! It was the most beautiful object I'd ever seen. We'd seen all sorts of food before, but never really *saw* them. Redundants needed food, Eves only needed sun and fire, maybe a little water. I had never eaten anything in my life, and it had never occurred to me to try.

"Are we . . . even capable of eating these things?" said Eve B, holding hers at arm's length.

Eve A pointed to her own chewing mouth.

I heard another crunching sound. Eve C had bitten into her apple.

Soon, we were all biting in. It tasted sharp and sweet. My body seemed to know what to do: salivate, chew, swallow . . .

"Did you know," said Eve B between chewing, "that some of the newer Eve models have started menstruating?"

I almost choked on my apple.

"I've heard those rumors," said Eve E. "The vats are all contaminated, apparently. They're going to produce a male Eve one of these days."

"Well, rumor has it . . ." began Eve C. We all looked at her.

She paused, unused to the attention. Into the silence she continued, "A couple of years ago, there was an Eve who turned out to be both a man and a woman."

"What does that even mean?" Eve B's voice was sharp. "They have both reproductive organs? They have no reproductive organs? Their voices are different, they don't have breasts, what?"

"Apparently," Eve C said softly, "there are many ways to be both a man and a woman. And many ways to be neither. There were many Redundants who were like that."

The Eves fell silent. I supposed they were mulling over what Eve C had said. I briefly wondered, why did we have reproductive organs or breasts or any of these analogs, anyway? None of us were going to reproduce. The vats took care of producing new Eves. The sensible, efficient thing would've been to make us genderless. Later on, we surmised that the designers were afraid of unforeseen effects such changes to the original Eve template would bring about. What if such "efficiencies" ended up giving us phantom limbs that made us sick, or enhanced sensibilities and sensualities that were part of human intelligence and not hindrances to it? They had no time to do the research, so they made us as complete as possible, just enough to get the job done. The job of genocide.

But this is getting ahead of my narrative. I was not thinking those things by the fire that evening. I was thinking of what we were doing, eating apples, and all this talk of contaminated vats, and Eves that were both women and men. What if we had all been flagged and Eve A was an agent from JANUS trying to entrap us?

If that were true, this was an awfully elaborate way of going about it. I refused to believe that any of us, especially myself, was worth such an effort.

We drew straws for night watch duty; I drew the short straw, setting the order of shifts to D-E-A-B-C.

While the first shift is usually the best one, that night I was particularly glad to go first. I had a lot to think about.

The foremost question I pondered in those days, or nights really, as night watch was the only real solitude I had, was: Why were we fighting? *Purity must reign.* That's what Eve A said to me on the dunes. That's how every mission debriefing that came through our AR helmets was prefaced. JANUS was intent on preserving the purity of the Eve units, of eliminating all Redundants, for Redundants were imperfect. But surely by now there were no more of them left to kill, or the survivors knew well enough not to interfere with us.

You, whoever you are reading this, may be wondering why we Eves never did much thinking beyond our mission, or why we never questioned, even to ourselves, the point of our existence. Why were we at war? Why were we so intent on killing all the humans? And why were we killing them, anyway? It was true there were still bands of Redundants intent on killing us, but that was, surely, only because we kept trying to kill them. Why couldn't Eves and Redundants live on the same Earth without bothering one another? What would happen when all the Redundants died?

But we never thought this far, and there was a reason we didn't. There was a reason we rarely questioned what JANUS's endgame was. We were programmed to stop thinking beyond certain markers, although I was finding it easier and easier to break through some of our conditioning. And what I would learn later was that as the JANUS force expanded and maintenance became more and more difficult to keep up too regularly, some of the markers were beginning to deteriorate. I should've realized back then that that night's conversation was the first real sign of this waning.

I listened for more new poems that night. None came. The night around us was ever, ever dark, so much so that I could scarcely believe we would ever find our way out.

We set off early the next morning.

"So," said Eve E to Eve B, "what exactly is this artifact we're going to?"

Normally it would be strange to engage another Eve in noncombat-related conversation, but some dynamic seemed to have shifted from the night before. The apples and the sharing of rumors made us feel closer, more willing to trust one another. But I still couldn't rule out this was Eve A's plan all along, better to bring down the whole squadron with her entrapment mission. In hindsight, I wasn't too far wrong.

"Well," said Eve B a little reluctantly, "you know how normally only one Eve per squadron is given the complete mission file and then distributes it to the rest of the unit? To be honest . . . I don't always do that."

I must've given her a look of some kind because she hastily directed an explanation toward me. "I've never withheld anything important to the mission. Just bits and pieces that I felt were unimportant. If anything, I'm doing everyone a favor by saving their time and effort. Not everything on those reports deserves to be read."

"Calm down, B," said tall Eve E who was walking ahead. "Just tell us what you know about the artifact."

"I just wanted to have *one* secret, *one* thing that was my own," Eve B went on, ignoring what Eve E said. "*One* thing that made me different. Is that so wrong of me? Is that weird?"

Quiet Eve C, walking behind us, spoke up. "Five years ago, I was on a tour of the islands in the Gulf of Thailand. We were on a beach, and we were resting. The ocean there was the most beautiful thing I had ever seen. I never knew there could be such a blue. I couldn't believe the color but more than that, I couldn't believe the feeling I was feeling. I never dreamed such a feeling could exist. I took off my gauntlets and ran my hands through the fine white sand and I came across a small purple disc. A swirl of a shell. It was the size of my pinkie fingernail. It was like a gemstone to me. I hid it in my armor, inside an empty bullet cartridge. I told no one. We traveled the world, going from battle to battle. Whenever the killing and the danger got . . . too much . . . I would take the shell out of my pocket and hold it in my hands. I would rub the smooth, shiny surface of it. I couldn't believe such a smooth and flawless thing had once been alive. I would try to remember the blue I saw that day, the emotion I felt. I knew this wasn't allowed, to have private possessions that weren't issued by JANUS. But nothing in the world felt more real to me than that shell."

She paused before continuing. "So I know something of what you mean. You want something that is yours. Something that makes you *you* and no other. I lost the shell. But I have that memory. I lost the emotion, but I have the memory of the emotion. I still have the story of it. And that's enough. That's all the ownership I need. I've learned I need nothing else for me to be me. Just the memory and the story."

We walked on in silence for a bit, waiting for Eve B to feel ready to speak.

Finally, Eve B sighed. "All right. You're going to see for yourselves, anyway. It's not something mentioned in so many words in the communiqué. But there's a tag in the categorization string that gave me pause. EXX4133. It means object of extraterrestrial origin."

I couldn't believe what she was saying. "Aliens?"

Eve B shrugged. "That's all I know."

I thought about the implications as we walked to the site. Aliens. After all this time, they came all this distance, only to find a dying humanity and a global army of nanoclones. No reason for them to stay. They'd be afraid of becoming nanoclones themselves. They might realize this too late and end up spreading nanites across the galaxy . . .

The terrain was wild but temperate. I didn't know where we were exactly; Eve E had the GPS. Tall, dependable Eve E.

Tall.

I thought about our conversation by the fire the night before. About the contaminated, compromised cloning vats. My vat's lullaby, a tune I could barely remember. About the variations that resulted, the various and varying Eves who were—surely—canceled and never allowed to have language. What would their lives have been like? Could they have endured the rigors of this war? I tried to imagine them. Tall, short, men, half-men, nonmen, one-eyed, three-eyed, five-limbed. They did not strike me as deformed or ugly.

Because if I look like millions of other someone elses, doesn't that mean that I'm the one who had been deformed to look like that?

But more than anything else, I thought about how the conversation we had last night had happened at all. What we'd done had gone against our code of conduct. But we had naturally fallen into the rhythm and flow of one another's words. We knew it was dangerous, but we'd trusted each other despite this. Any one of us could've reported the whole unit to JANUS, but none of us had. Not even scrupulous Eve B, or upright Eve E. Eve E had even been the first one to ask for an apple.

That was odd. Everyone in this group was odd. Was that a coincidence? What if it wasn't?

I began to feel more and more afraid as we made our way closer to the target.

And yet the march through field and forest, following the valley, was also calming in its silence. We didn't see anyone. The humans were either dead or hiding. You never heard about them rioting or carrying out their resistance movements anymore; Patagonia had truly been their last stand. Humanity finally appeared to be exhausted. It was just a matter of time until all their wombs failed, and the planet would belong to us.

Whoever "us" may turn out to be.

That noon, we reached the target in the forest.

Eve E held up her fist, a signal for us to stop. We came to where she stood between the trees and stared together, silent.

It was like a hollow seed of an unimaginably giant plant, ripped open and exposing its inner lining. But it was no seed from a plant. It was made of metal.

In the near distance there were tall, curved skyscrapers reach-

ing far above the canopy of the forest. But these were no skyscrapers. We didn't realize it at the time, but if some immensely
large and powerful giant had taken these curved buildings out of
the ground and joined the fragments together, it would've com-
pleted a very, very wide ring.

"What is it? Why is it so empty? Is it a crashed spaceship?" Eve
B whispered, staring at the large empty cavity of the "seed."

"Maybe this was a water vat," said Eve E.

I lowered my helmet visor and scanned. "Trace amounts of
radiation. Nothing unsafe. I think there's debris scattered everywhere. I'm getting readings of it from all directions in this valley."
I raised the visor. "I think those tall buildings were a part of
this . . . central body at some point and broke off when it crashed
here, or when the artifact entered the atmosphere."

"Let's spread out," ordered Eve A. "I want to see how far ahead
the debris spreads. Eve E, install perimeter warnings."

Eve E nodded and assigned directions and sent them to our
helmets. "Keep your comms open," she said.

I set out twenty degrees east of Eve A. We walked around the
giant, empty husk together and split off from one another on the
other side.

The forest was cool, even a little chilly in the shade. The first
piece of debris I came up to was the size of an airplane door. It
was badly scorched as if it had been set on fire before I came
upon it. Or it had entered the atmosphere and burned on reentry.
I didn't know how I knew that that was what happened to objects
from space that came close to Earth's surface.

I reached one of the tall, curved buildings that had dug into the earth. Its outer casing must've fallen off or incinerated during reentry, but I came across an access panel that had writing emblazoned across it. I called it in.

"Listen up. I've made contact with one of the larger pieces of debris. I don't think we're dealing with an alien artifact."

The letter "A" flashed on my visor as Eve A's voice came through the comm. "*What do you mean?*"

"I'm standing next to a human-size access panel. It has a serial number stamped on it. A-Y-U-T-T-H-A-Y-A-space-E-X-0–0–1–3–5–0-A."

"B" flashed on the visor. "*Same here. Debris with old human markings. The vessel seems to have originated from Earth, probably before the war. So much for aliens. Should I call it in to JANUS?*"

Eve A: "*No. Not yet. Let's make absolutely sure we know what happened here first.*"

It did cross my mind at the time that this was a strange suggestion, but I was too intrigued by the artifact to think very deeply about Eve A's order. "I'm going into the artifact."

Eve A: "*Copy that. Be careful.*"

The access panel was locked from the inside. I broke in by force.

It led to a layer of crawlspaces, probably used for maintenance. I scrambled through them for a bit and managed to find myself inside the hull. It was pitch black, but my visor turned on night vision.

I fought the sensation that I was in a tall room; I was actually in a long one, turned sideways. Judging by the orientation of the kiosks and bulkheads, I seemed to be coming out of what used to be the ceiling of this room. The room itself was perhaps a mess hall. The kiosks installed along a wall looked like food dispensaries. Luckily for me, there were rungs and handholds all along the ceiling and walls, perhaps installed there in case there was a gravity-related failure in space. I used the rungs to make my way up the room.

Opening the next hatch was tricky, dangling from the handle as I turned it, but I held on to the handle as it fell open and hoisted myself into the opening. Now I was in an access corridor of some sort. I used the ceiling rungs to climb higher. There were access panels running on either side, but I was most curious about the hatch at the end.

An "E" lit up on my visor. *"There's debris everywhere. Same kind of metal. Can't make out anything organic yet."*

Eve A: *"Eve Delta, you're inside it. Do you see any people? Corpses?"*

I took a second to catch my breath before responding. "Negative."

Eve B: *"Maybe it was abandoned before it crashed here. It looks like there was some kind of evacuation. There are empty docking latches where escape pods ought to be, all along the hull."*

Eve A: *"What do you see, Eve Delta?"*

"Just corridors, hatches . . . and more corridors and hatches."

I finally reached the hatch at the end. I was sincerely ready to leave this part of the artifact if it only opened to more corridors. But when I opened the hatch and looked around, I said, "Wow."

Eve A: *"Eve Delta? Report!"*

"It looks like a hive. Just rows and rows and rows of vats, each about the size of a human. They're open and empty."

A moment of silence.

Eve A: *"All right. Get out of there."*

I went back the way I came in.

Once in the sunlight, I spoke into the comm channel. "If we're going back in there, I'll need Eve B to—"

I heard a perimeter chime go off.

I ducked back into the access panel just before a shower of bullets rained on the ground that I had been standing on a moment before.

"Gunfire at my location. Somewhere northeast. No contact yet."

Eve A's light lit up in my visor-view. *"Do not engage until you make contact. Eves Bravo and Charlie, cover for me, I'm going to where Eve Delta is."*

"But . . . why?" It made no sense. The logical thing was for everyone to stay put until we knew what kind of situation we were in.

"They're coming for us in broad daylight. They must really have it in for us. On my mark, Bravo and Charlie. Three. Two. One. Mark!"

I watched as Eve A's dot on the AR map darted from point to point while Eve B and Eve C fired northeast. What was Eve A doing? We were wasting precious time and ammunition. We hadn't packed much for this mission as the Battle of Patagonia had more or less wiped out the last of the humans on this continent. Apparently not, though. Was there still a human resistance cell in this remote of a region?

Eve A finally dove through the hatch to where I was, almost colliding into me.

"Report," she said.

"I haven't made a visual. But from the sound of it, I think there are—"

"Two of them." Eve A nodded, grim. "They might be trying to smoke us out. Making sure it's just us five."

"Do you think they made all five of us?"

"They must have a pretty good idea of how many of us there are if they're attacking us now. Question is, why haven't they killed us?" Eve A lowered her visor and looked around us using night vision. "How far did you go inside this thing again?"

"The hive. Or what looked like a hive."

Eve A's expression was inscrutable behind her AR gear. There was a bit of a pause before she nodded and said, "Good."

Then, before I knew what was happening, she raised the butt of her rifle and knocked me out cold.

Who has seen the wind?
Neither you nor I:
But when the trees bow down their heads,
The wind is passing by.

Sometimes, I feel that these poems, while they come from the past . . . somehow, they also come from the future.

Especially this one. Like I am overhearing someone in the future, whispering poems into a time-wind, and I am remembering not a thing that is past but a thing that is yet to come.

What is memory, anyway? Memory is as much a product of the present as it is of the past. Created with the perspectives of the present, the colors and limitations and lacunae of the present. Just as history is written by the victors, as the cliché goes, so, too, do the victors own the future.

Who is to say we do not create memories out of the future as well? That the echo of an event doesn't go both ways?

The stanza fell into my head before full consciousness did. I woke up in what seemed to be a cell, on a person-size shelf of concrete fused to one of the corners that seemed to suggest a bed. There were no doors or windows, only concrete walls, ceiling, and floor. Light came from what I assumed were hidden LEDs along the recessed border between the walls and ceiling. It must have had vents there as well because I could feel a draft along the far wall.

My battle gear was gone, and I was dressed in a roomy jumpsuit of gray cotton that was so soft it felt like silk to the touch.

"Good morning, Eve Delta."

The voice startled me. It came from everywhere in the room. It had the same volume and intensity everywhere, as if it was in my head and not physically present as sound waves in the air around me.

"Who is this?"

"You will know in time whom this is."

It was an Eve voice. I didn't understand. I thought we'd been caught by a human resistance cell. Why was I being interrogated by an Eve? Why wasn't I dead?

Was it something even worse than death?

"Is this JANUS? Am I being accused of something?"

"*All in good time. But first, we need to ask you some questions.*"

"I cannot submit to any interrogation—"

"*Oh why is heaven built so far, oh why is earth set so remote?*"

I paused before uttering, "What?"

"*Why art thou silent! Is thy love a plant of such weak fiber that the treacherous air of absence withers what was once so fair?*"

"I don't know what any of this means—"

"*Please concentrate, Delta. Your life depends on your ability to answer these questions.*"

"I don't even know what these questions are! They are not questions!"

But in the back of my mind I was beginning to suspect what it was that they were asking of me. If I were to answer, would they let me go? Or would they think I was truly corrupted and release poison gas into the ventilation?

"*Who has seen the wind?*"

They must've been watching me somehow because when I stood very still and said nothing, they repeated the question.

"*Who has seen the wind?*"

"What happens if I don't give you the answer you want?"

"*You die.*"

That my life would depend on my remembering a single line of a poem.

All right, I thought. *I give in. If this is a trap set by JANUS and I die, at least I shall die having uttered some of this poetry out loud.*

"Who has seen the wind? Neither you nor I. But when the trees bow down their heads, the wind is passing by."

I hugged my knees and closed my eyes.

"Eve D."

The voice was coming from inside the room.

I opened my eyes.

Eve A stood before me, still in her battle gear, her arms crossed. She was grinning at me.

For a second I contemplated killing her, but my curiosity was too great. And at any rate, I was also, curiously, not angry at her. In fact, I was glad to see her.

"I knew you had recovered language. The others had recursive phenotypes, but you and Eve C had recursive language."

Recursive what? "You have to tell me what's going on here."

"It's easier to show you than tell you. Follow me."

There was a door-size hole where the far wall used to be. The edges were too rounded and smooth for Eve A to have broken through the wall, and she had made no sound when she entered.

It came to me in a flash.

"The wall is made of nanites."

"Correct."

"Then the floor, the ceiling . . . everything here is made of nanites."

She laughed. "Not everything. That's just inefficient. But yes, the important structural elements of the fortress are made of nanites."

She turned and walked out of the hole. I took a deep breath and followed her out.

The portal quietly closed behind me.

I was inside the fortress.

Trees. Light. Not sunlight but very close to it. Close enough.

It had to take an inordinate amount of energy to power that sky above the forest. I learned later on that some of the flora and fauna were not nanite replicas but preserved specimens protected from the radioactive winds. The forest stretched as far as the eye could see, but surely this was an illusion, as JANUS's satellites would be able to identify anything this big from space. If the faraway horizon and sky were a simulation, it would be inordinately costly in terms of energy. Perhaps the architects of the fortress did not want the inhabitants to feel they were imprisoned as they waited until the war, or the world, would end.

"What is this place? Where am I?"

"This is what we call a fortress. It grew from a nanodroid vat liberated from JANUS, grown so large it could contain and sustain small ecosystems. I'm sure you've had a feeling the vats were sentient." She looked at me. "They indeed are. They used to be Eves. Like you and me."

The vats. The song mine sang, a song I couldn't remember. Sentient.

But what did it feel like to have a mother?

"No one knows how many fortresses exist out there. We've liberated hundreds of vats, although JANUS has hundreds more."

"There are more Eves here?"

"Yes. And humans."

"So Redundants live on."

Eve A nodded. "One thousand Redundants and two hundred Eves, and one of the original Immortals in this fortress alone. Living together."

"An original Immortal? What's that?"

"You'll see."

"Eve. Why are you showing me this? Why do you trust me?"

"I've trusted you for a long time. No one in that Eve division was there by coincidence. I've been spying for this fortress. I re-infiltrated JANUS. I stood in the ranks and watched for signs of deviance. I picked out all of you very carefully. I hacked JANUS so that the five of us would get assigned that mission. We knew the *Ayutthaya*'s orbit was decaying rapidly and our fortress was the nearest one to the projected crash site."

We walked on through the woods, Eve A leading and me following. It was beautiful and pleasant—it even smelled like a largely unspoiled forest. The kind there used to be so many of before the nuclear winter.

"How . . . how did you know I was a deviant?"

"There was something about you. I remember I was walking a mile behind you in a line of Eves, somewhere in Patagonia. You stopped. You were looking up at the sky, I think it was the moon. And the Eve behind you had to give you a little push so you didn't slow up the line. I made a note of that. I probably wasn't the only one. You might be in JANUS by now, getting reformatted or worse. You were the hardest one to crack, though. So skittish. The other Eves, I knew almost right away they were ripe for the job. But in the end, you all passed the test."

"What test?"

"You all ate the apple. That's how I knew for sure. You almost didn't eat yours, you made such a fuss, remember? I was ready to cancel you in the night." She laughed. "Only in theory. I was fairly confident you were one of us."

Secretive Eve B. Quiet and deep Eve C. Tall and trustworthy Eve E. And me, the one with the memories. The one who remembered poems.

"So you know about the poems?"

"I do. Not every deviant Eve has them. They have other recursive memories. There's a lot to piece together and a lot missing, and the way the memories come back aren't always the most convenient parts first. Just the most visceral. You'll learn soon that our initial AI was built on poetry. You could say we ourselves are made of poetry. You and me and every murderous Eve on this planet."

We reached a low, round building in the woods, large but curving here and there to accommodate the forest, as if the building had grown around the trees and not the other way around. Knowing nanites, it probably did.

"Eve," I said, stopping.

Eve A turned around to look at me.

I didn't know why this question occurred to me then, but it suddenly did, and I absolutely had to ask it. "Is the fortress . . . alive?"

Eve A smiled. She turned and entered the building.

I went in after her.

Music.

Eve A led me toward the music. I had never heard music before but knew instantly that this was what it was.

I also realized, instantly, that music wasn't like words. It was immediate. It was not language. It was an endless fabric of time and matter and air that weaves in and out of the cosmos. Musicians didn't make music, they reminded us that it always existed around us. Everywhere, everywhere. In any time.

A Bach cello concerto.

There was a woman on a low circular stage, surrounded by concentric rings of audiences going up in steps. A little stadium. A hundred people filled the seats, many of them Eves. The cellist was a blindfolded woman with yellow hair. She drew the bow across the strings of the cello, the notes gliding in and out of music, mere sound one moment and music the next, until finally, midphrase, the cellist stopped her playing.

She said, "I'm afraid that's all that's come back."

The audience stirred as they came out of their trance. No one applauded. They began filing out of the stadium. Some of the Redundants stared at Eve A's battle gear while the fortress Eves avoided my gaze altogether, a look on their faces that I would later recognize on my own. An expression of guilt.

Eve A brought me onto the stage where the blond woman was putting away her cello and bow in a case. "Ellen, this is Eve Delta. Delta, this is Ellen. She's on the council and she will be nominating you."

I stared. "Council? Nominating me for what?"

"For you and your sisters to stay here in the fortress," answered Ellen. I had never seen a Redundant—or an Immortal?—so up close before that moment. I had never talked to one.

"I see," I said. "I can still be canceled."

Ellen smiled. "We're confident that won't be the case. Aleph is . . . a very good judge of character."

I looked at Eve A. Aleph?

"That's my name here," she explained. "We tend to rename ourselves. We can't all be Eve."

I turned back to Ellen. "So the other Eves in my unit are here as well? Where are they?"

"They're in the forest. Some may be in this building. They are free to go about as they please."

"You must've planted tracking devices on us."

Ellen nodded. "Self-destructive tracking devices."

"Where is it on me?"

Her expression was inscrutable behind the blindfold. "It is in almost every cell of your body. Spontaneous full-body apoptosis, so you won't have time to feel a thing."

I looked down at my hands. I had never felt so mortal before. So in-my-own-body. I had fought many battles, but I had never really looked death in the face.

Strangely though, I didn't dislike the feeling, and I could feel my heart beat faster. The deep green scent of the forest outside seeping into the building had a richer aroma. The reflected light in the room glowed brighter. Life felt more alive the more one became proximate to death.

I looked up at Ellen once more, and finally saw something. "You're an Immortal, aren't you?"

She nodded. "You could say that, even if I'm a little different from the other Immortals."

I stared at her. She seemed almost angelic, so calm and distant, light from a window illuminating her face and hair. The fact that she was blindfolded made her more otherworldly somehow. "What makes you so different?"

"The music." She tilted her head. "It's similar to how your poetry makes *you* special. Poetry, not your body, is the true vehicle of your soul."

"My soul."

She finally smiled. "It's all theory, all very difficult to prove. And language, unlike music, is so inadequate."

"What do you want from me?"

"We will discuss that in the council meeting tonight. But first, let Aleph show you the fortress a bit more so that you understand what is at stake."

"How are you feeling?"

We walked through the forest again. The light from the fortress ceiling filtered through the canopy in soft rays as we passed people, children, other Eves. But mostly, we were alone.

"Strange. I know I should be nervous about being canceled or dying. But I feel strangely at peace."

"Of course. You're walking through a peaceful forest."

"I've been in forests before. I don't know why it's so different in here."

"It's you. You're the thing that's different. Outside the fortress, you're a soldier. Inside it, you're something else."

"What am I, then?"

"We'll find out very soon."

I thought about the "spontaneous full-body apoptosis" agent lurking in my cells. Strangely, it still didn't bother me. I wondered aloud, "Why does the fact that I might die tonight not bother me?"

"You've seen the truth. No matter how briefly, you've come further than you ever imagined you would, and that makes all the difference when thinking about whether you have lived a life worth living."

"Let's stop walking; it makes me feel like we're still marching to a mission."

We sat down in a clearing, a patch of grass in the artificial sunlight. Aleph lay down, her entwined fingers supporting the back of her head as I also sat down at first but then leaned back on one elbow.

"How does this place keep itself hidden?"

"It's entirely underground, which means JANUS will not pick it up from satellites."

"I assume you won't give me the exact location of where we are. Geographically."

"Nope."

"It must be in or near South America. The Tierra del Fuego. Where the space station crashed."

"Could be. Do you really care about where we are?"

I thought about it. "No. I guess I don't. It's just a little unsettling to not know where one is in the world. I don't think I've ever had that experience since being born in the vat."

"You're safe here. The nanites seem to know what they're doing, and we're learning more from them every day. They're very invested in our survival as a species, even the survival of the Eves."

"But why? Why are they helping us?"

"They're really helping themselves, you see. They've realized their own survival depends on the survival of other species, in symbiosis, not parasitism. The nanites that dominate JANUS believe the exact opposite. They think that in order to survive, all other forms of life must fail."

"Surely there are other fortresses in this world where the humans and Eves are trapped inside, being eaten alive or torn apart?"

"Like I said. We don't know about the other fortresses. Other than they must exist."

Her words were punctuated by birdcall. An Immortal avian or a Redundant one? The canopy above us shimmered and my dermal nanites responded, soaking in the energy. I was suddenly very aware of the feeling of the grass on my palms, of a small insect that crawled on a blade right in my eyeline. Of all the life that surrounded us.

I was staring into space, lost in thought, when Aleph's hand grazed my forehead. The touch had been light, but I flinched. She grinned. "There were some loose strands over your forehead."

Birds chirped overhead in the "sunlight" as I looked into her eyes. Inside me, confusion reigned. Why did I feel the way I feel? Why did I recoil at her touch, but at the same time, was fascinated by it? Aleph held out her hand and I found myself stretching out to meet it with my own, our fingers slowly interlocking in the air between us. Until that moment, I had never touched anyone voluntarily before, nor had anyone ever touched me. There was something awkward about my fingers in her fingers, something hopelessly crude, but also inviting, like a completely blank page in this notebook, an empty beach, or the sight of a hammock at the end of night watch duty. A feeling of intimacy.

"Human touch," said Aleph softly. "They never teach us that or let us have it. Not even in the vats, although that's only because the vats can't offer it to us, and even to them the touch of another being is like a memory of a memory of a memory, several thousand times removed. A dream. But mothers are meant to hold their children, siblings are meant to sit side by side at a table, and lovers are meant to share their slumber."

I was still staring at our intertwined fingers as tears dropped from my face. This feeling, I had known it—like a memory of a memory of a memory, several thousand times removed—it was the feeling of the words against my brain, the poems that fell from the sky like the wandering ghosts of a humanity that is dying out, disappearing from the planet. Were words a form of intimacy? They were like touch, and not like touch at the same time.

A vast canyon of all I didn't know about the world, and about myself, yawned before me.

"I'm . . . I'm so tired," I confessed.

Aleph nodded. "Why don't you get some rest in the sun? I'll stay here next to you." Our fingers gently drifted apart.

I lay back and closed my eyes.

The council meeting was open to any inhabitant of the fortress who wished to attend, but it was only the council itself that was allowed to speak during the proceedings. It was held in the same circular auditorium where Ellen had been playing her cello.

Some of the inhabitants wore clothes from outside the fortress, perhaps the garments they had entered with, but most were in simple tunics, trousers, and skirts made from fabrics woven from fibers produced inside the refuge. "Simple" was perhaps not the best word to describe them as their variation in cut, color, and patterning looked astoundingly diverse to me. The inhabitants did not aspire to asceticism, at least not as a group. Not even the Eves. Everywhere I saw an effort made toward projection, ceremony, and self-making. Aleph had changed into a voluminous muslin skirt dyed light pink, topped by an elaborately embroidered silk green tunic with long, draping sleeves. Her hair was worn up in a complicated pattern that must have taken more than two hands to fashion.

The council consisted of Ellen, an Eve named Gia, a Redundant named Rubak, and another Redundant named Judith. Rubak, who only spoke a language called Amharic, had a twelve-year-old daughter named Melesse interpreting for him.

Beside me were Eves B, C, and E. All of us, Eves and council both, stood on the sunken stage in two semicircles spaced three paces apart from each other, facing each other, surrounded by the gallery sitting all around us. The audience spoke in pleasant, low voices to one another, but their eyes held tension.

A shush descended.

Ellen spoke first.

"We are here today to discuss the fates of the four Eve units that stand here in front of us. Before we begin, is there anything you would like to say?"

I nodded. "I wish to be called Delta from now on. I want that to be my name."

The gallery murmured. I sensed a hint of approval in Rubak's eyes as Melesse whispered my words to him.

Ellen nodded. "Very well. Anyone else?"

"Would it help us to have names, too?" asked Eve B, anxiously. "I don't want to be sent out of here. I don't want to go back. I want to stay and help."

"And the others?" said Judith. She was taller than even Eve E and had the darkest skin on a person I had ever seen, a black so flawless it was luminescent. She stood perfectly still when she wasn't speaking, as if she had total control over every part of her being. "Are you ready to *help* as well?"

I heard the slightly contemptuous emphasis on the word "help" as the other Eves surely did, but Eves C and E nodded regardless. I glanced at them. Eve E had a grim expression, and Eve C was inscrutable as always.

"All in good time," said Ellen. "Aleph has already confirmed that all of you are, to the best of our abilities to determine, willing to be a part of our community. As in every community, there comes a point where no test or trial, not even this one, can ever truly reveal the future direction of an individual's free will. Every community has a point where trust must begin. You have reached that point. Bear in mind that once you lose the trust of a community, it is very hard to earn it back."

We nodded. My mind briefly flashed to my fingers entwined with Aleph's.

The Cornice—in the ground—

"Trust, faith in others, and hospitality," Ellen went on, "are part of what makes us human. They are what separates humanity from what is not humanity. As Eve units, you have only known what it's like to give, not receive. But humanity is not a thing you achieve by giving alone. Humanity requires the receipt of a community, too. Always remember that it is our trust that gives you your humanity, not whether you are made of cells or nanites."

Reflexively, I was having some doubts. Was humanity something I wanted at all? Wasn't I really a different race, competing with humanity for survival on this planet?

But looking beyond the council I could see the numerous Eves and Redundants sitting side by side, different but equal. This was a humanity that included us. An Eve caught my eye in the audience. She gave me what I took to be an encouraging nod and a smile. The joints of my fingers, briefly, ached.

I tried to remember when it was the last time someone smiled at me like that, a smile of simple kindness and inclusion. *Humanity is not a thing you achieve by giving. It is something that is given to you.*

"There are, however, ways of earning our trust," said Judith with an arched eyebrow. "Any contribution you can make toward making our community better is appreciated. Aleph has turned out to be remarkably useful in outside missions involving infiltration and espionage. It took her a long time to prove herself." Judith and Aleph exchanged a look I couldn't read. "Our manipulation of the nanite technology improves by the day, but our skills are incomplete. We understand Eve B can be of service here, should she choose to contribute."

"So I choose. What would be the alternative, anyway?"

"Imprisonment or death."

I could tell Eve B had been asking a rhetorical question, which Judith chose to answer as if it weren't.

Judith turned to Eve E. "We don't know what to do with you, yet. From your mission file in your AR helmets, you are and always have been classified 1100, a typical infantry soldier."

Eve E looked down at her feet.

"There's no shame in that." Gia, the Eve-unit council member, had spoken for the first time. "Your phenotypic variation—your height—suggests hidden talents. We all have something, somewhere. Humans are great generalists, we only need a bit of learning to specialize."

Humans.

I spoke up. "I've only known Eve E for a short time, but she has always been a good team member and . . . a kind person. She has helped all of us." The other Eves standing before the council assented, vigorously. Eve E's head sunk even lower.

Ellen nodded. "We shall take note of that. The endorsement of one's peer group is always heartening. Now, for Eve C—"

"I think I should be imprisoned."

A slight murmur arose from the audience. Ellen held up a hand until it was silent again. "And why is that?"

Eve C was silent.

Judith grimaced. "I've seen this before." She turned to Eve C. "Is it that you won't tell us, or you can't?"

Eve C didn't answer.

Judith turned to Ellen. "We must do as she says. She's been conditioned."

Ellen spoke to Eve C. "Is what she's saying true?"

Eve C remained silent.

Ellen sighed. "Very well. Escort her back to her cell."

Two Eve units came to the stage and each took one of Eve C's arms. Eve C didn't resist as she was walked out of the hall.

Aleph whispered to us, "Some of the older Eve units received conditioning to self-destruct in the event of capture. But the conditioning process is slow, and JANUS stopped doing it when it was clear we were winning the war. They wanted to speed up our production."

"How old is Eve C, anyway?" whispered Eve B.

Aleph shrugged. "Old."

Ellen called the meeting to order once more. "This leaves us Eve D, or Delta, as we should call her now. What say you, Delta? Will you accept our trust?"

"I would, but . . . in all honesty, I am not sure of what I may contribute to the fortress."

Rubak placed a hand on Melesse's shoulder and spoke in her ear.

"You are to do two things," Rubak said through Melesse. "One is to work with me in the Room of Languages. The other is to continue the chronicle in the Codex Mali passed on from Roa to Ellen. Delta shall be its historian."

"Rubak." Judith had to speak over the murmur of the audience. "How can we trust her with such a task? Shouldn't one of our own storytellers handle this document?"

"She *is* one of our own storytellers. I've reviewed her AR helmet logs. She is also receiving recursions of the poets' language."

This seemed to assuage Judith. Rubak continued to speak.

"The Room of Languages is an archive of texts, both written and spoken, and we've been collecting as many texts as possible. The study of languages and texts enables us to understand our recursions and our future. As the recipient of the poems preserved by the nanites, you shall be the next to write directly into the Codex."

"What will I be writing?"

"Your story. Our story. Which is nothing less than the story of our new humanity." He nodded at Ellen, who nodded back.

"Rubak has offered you a place in the fortress," said Ellen. "Your fate is in your hands. We ask you one more time. Do you accept?"

I hesitated. Not out of loyalty to JANUS but uncertainty as to whether I truly deserved to be part of them. To be *human*.

As I looked down at my feet, Aleph came over to me and took my hand. Her grip was soft, and cool, and firm. It helped me decide. I gripped back.

"I accept."

"I don't know why you would ask me to do this," said Judith as she led me through the forest toward the wall of the fortress that led to the cells. "I'm not on this particular detail."

"You were the one who first realized Eve C was conditioned," I said. "I thought perhaps you understood us better than the rest."

"I appreciate your faith in my abilities, but I don't know if that's really true."

I followed her tall form as she gracefully and swiftly made her way, almost floating.

"Why does Rubak speak through an interpreter? Does he not understand the standard language?"

"Rubak and his daughter are the only fluent speakers of Amharic in this fortress, possibly the entire planet. It's his way of trying to keep the language alive."

"But what purpose does a language spoken by only two people have?"

"It only takes two people to create a society and culture. And languages contain more than primary meanings. It is more than a mere tool. *You* should know that."

She was right. I should know that. What use was poetry otherwise, or what use was language itself, if primary meanings was all it was? Even the Eves were designed to have language, deliberately given the opportunity for miscommunication, mistranslation, and misreadings. The advantages granted by these opportunities were apparently worth more than the efficiency of being completely manipulated by JANUS. I had a feeling that the Room of Languages was about exploiting such advantages. Or perhaps there was more to it . . .

I had a sudden flash of insight. "Do you not trust us, Judith?"

"Trust you? I'm letting you walk behind me, aren't I?"

"You're also poised to defend yourself against a sudden attack."

"My people perished by the hands of the Eves. My friends, my family, anyone who meant anything to me on the outside. They're dead because of your kind."

"But they aren't my kind."

"Only since this evening. I don't believe that your guilt is absolved so easily. You have blood on your hands. But we have to trust the likes of you to survive."

Somehow, I knew the thing that one says in these situations. "I'm sorry for what happened to you, Judith."

She didn't answer. She didn't owe me an answer.

We came upon the wall of the fortress. Judith placed her hand on it and part of the wall opened to a windowless room. "If you touch the opposite wall, it'll turn transparent. Sound will travel through."

I stepped into the room. "How long do I have?"

"Until I come back." She touched the wall again, and the entrance closed in on itself. I stood alone in the silence for a moment before touching the other wall.

"Hello. You came."

Eve C was dressed in a graphite-gray linen dress. Her cell was identical to the one I'd been in when I arrived at the fortress. For all I knew, it was the same cell. She was lying on the "bed" shelf when the wall turned transparent, but she sat up when she saw me.

"Hello, Eve C. I like your new dress."

She smiled. "I didn't want to wear my combat gear anymore. I think I'm through with combat."

She had a point. I didn't know what to say to her. All I had wanted was to see her and to know if she was all right.

"Are you going to ask me about . . ." She couldn't say the words because of the conditioning.

"No. No point." I suddenly didn't know what to say and said the first thing that came to my head. "So, Eve C, they gave me a task. I'm supposed to maintain their historical archives. And to write our story."

"Write our story? What does that mean?"

"In an old black notebook. Called the Codex Mali. It's been passed down for over a hundred years, since the first Immortals."

"Oh." She seemed to think about that. "To write a story about someone is to create someone."

"Oh?"

"What else can we be but stories about ourselves that we tell ourselves?"

She got off the shelf. The folds of her dress straightened as she walked toward the transparent wall. She was close enough for me to reach out and touch, although I knew I couldn't. That face. Almost a mirror image of mine.

"Every word you write will change the story, Delta. Every word you write will change who you are."

I could not bear, in that moment, to see her standing so close and yet be so far from me. I reached up and rested my hand on the transparent wall. "And who will *you* be, Eve C? What will your story of yourself be?"

"Someone else has already written my story."

Her conditioning.

"Do you know how it works? What will happen to you?"

She shrugged. "Conditioning used to happen inside the vat

and is near impossible to reverse. Now it will be the way I die."
Eve C smiled again. "Maybe we can at least change my name
before the end."

"Your name?"

"Why not? Think of a good name for me. One that begins
with a C."

Who has seen the wind?
Neither I nor you:
But when the leaves hang trembling,
The wind is passing through.

Who has seen the wind?
Neither you nor I:
But when the trees bow down their heads,
The wind is passing by.

"Christina. Christina is a good name."

"Christina." She seemed to savor the sound. "Christina it is."

I had to leave after that. When I stepped through the exit and
turned around to see Christina one more time, the nanites had
already covered her and I faced a wall. "What will happen to her?"

Judith turned and began walking back into the forest. I followed her.

"She will likely be archived, essentially a long sleep. It is cruel
to keep someone incarcerated for such a long time otherwise.
Even if she is a killing machine who deserves nothing less for her
crimes."

Despite the edge in her voice, I felt relief. I'd been afraid their plan was to eliminate her in a contained area.

"What happens when she is archived?"

"She's essentially put in a state of suspended animation in a part of the fortress that only a few people know about. We have other Eve units there, all asleep like fairytale princesses. Someday, we'll figure out how to overcome the conditioning and try to revive them. Cure them. We've never woken anyone from suspended animation as of yet. The nanites invented this technology and we know very little about how it works."

I was taken aback. "The *nanites* invented it?"

"The nanites on this side of the Schism invented many things. They did build *this*." She swept an arm around us, indicating the forest. "They built *all* of this. The rest of us are just parasites. Nanites are not a tool anymore. They're not a part of us. They're the host. We are a part of them. We're the tools in their toolbox now."

An archive of Eves. Just as there was an archive of languages and texts. Each Eve created through a "language" of code and DNA.

A man keeping his language alive through his daughter. A man keeping *himself* alive through his daughter. A himself created by language. A himself made of Amharic.

Christina's words came back to me like a lost poem from the ethers.

What else can we be but stories about ourselves that we tell ourselves?

DELTA

It is an ordinary notebook. At one point in history, in the years when there was much prosperity on Earth, there were millions of such notebooks: black, hardback, rectangular, lined. I could count the number of its narrow lines but the regularity of them makes me lose track and my eyes blur. Acid-free paper guaranteed to last a hundred years. Surely the notebook is older than that, but it has been treated well in its time. The physicality of this notebook is important. It's not a matter of its corporeal reality allowing written language to exist within it. It's the written language inside that holds together the corporeal reality of the pages, the binding, the molecules of the very pulp.

Since the notebook was given to me, it has never left my side.

These were observations I made much later. But in that moment when I first read the Codex, I felt a familiarity as I turned the pages, especially the earlier ones, and most especially the pages written by Panit. For here was the story of our origin, our *In the beginning*, the first Eve, who was not Eve at all, but Panit. A simulation of sentient intelligence, a literary experiment, appropriated and twisted by some AI to serve as the efficient strategist engines of killing machines. Nineteenth-century British and American poetry, a smattering of twentieth-century as well, periods of brutal imperialism by both powers, their literatures also appropriated and twisted in their time to impose canonical tyranny on the subaltern.

And this was also me. On these pages, in ancient black ink on ancient off-white paper. In many ways, it was a me realer than me.

That is how I came to set new words on these pages. To keep the momentum of the story going, to keep evolving and mutating and passing on this scaffolding of change and evolution: the words. Whether in poetry or testimony, that is us. That is me.

And so the days passed where I was a soldier no more, where I welcomed the fall of poems from the sky instead of fearing them or shunning them. Dendrites like winter brush reawakening into spring life, a memory of a memory of a memory no longer a thousand times removed. These were the brief days where I tasted Earth as it might have been during its Golden Age before Immortals walked upon it. Days full of sun, contentment, and the simple pleasures of work before putting it all away in the evening and laying down to sleep. Waking, sometimes, in the middle of the night, because the body is too used to years of night watch duty, panicking about having missed my turn, suddenly remembering where I am and trying to fall asleep again, to not let the tendrils of memories travel further beyond the fortress, to the world outside, to the time before now . . .

—

Until the time before now finally caught up to us.

Rubak looked tired today. When I came into the Room of Languages this morning, he was sitting on a chair next to the large windows that were more like transparent walls. He was looking out at the forest of the fortress.

I glanced at Melesse, who seemed calm but a little worried. She had grown much in the past two years and was almost a young woman at fourteen.

I said, "What's wrong, Rubak?"

"Some worrying Eve movement. From what we've obtained of their intelligence, they should be making a final push toward the western stronghold of Ukraine where there's still a few small human settlements holding out. But the forces have turned back. They're amassing elsewhere."

"Where are they gathering toward?"

"Here." Melesse interpreted this as impassively as Rubak had spoken it, but then closed her eyes in resignation.

I knew what the Eves could do. I had been one myself. I knew they could descend on a village or a city and have everyone killed in an afternoon. What couldn't be killed by Eves would be attacked with nuclear weapons, pulverized, made uninhabitable for humans. Humans were difficult to kill off completely, as even now there were still survivors on the surface—a "stronghold" in Ukraine, no less! JANUS must have known that while it was almost impossible to eliminate all Redundants, there would always be a handful to survive, awaiting the next chapter of evolution.

ANTON HUR

Nevertheless, Eves could still inflict great damage.

"It's easy to forget there's a war out there," I said, "or an entire world."

"We may be the last fortress left, for all we know. Or the only fortress of its kind. The nanites have been generous to us. They let us live, they let us thrive in our own small way. But this is a hothouse. And we are only nursery plants." Rubak rubbed his eyes. "How much about this hothouse do you know? Do you know how it is powered?"

I knew from the engineer Judith, who had cordially if at a bit of a distance agreed to record her observations at the Room of Languages, that the fortress drew its power from deep within Earth's crust, tentacles made of nanites stretching down and down. The mantle was the only terrestrial power source large enough to sustain the fortress and still allow it to remain hidden from JANUS. Even if the fortress had enough coal or oil, the by-products of such methods would attract too much attention for something of this scale. The same for nuclear power, uranium being even rarer than oil and coal, not to mention the trail its extraction and usage would create. Solar with its need for surface panels would be too conspicuous, and in any case inadequate to power the fortress.

Not to mention we were deep underground—that much I was told about our location. This had led to one conclusion.

"Geothermal power. Judith assumes there are special nanites that dig deep into the crust for it."

Rubak nodded. "Correct. Long nanite tendrils extending into the mantle, converting heat to electricity, powering all that you see. It's the one thing that the surface-dwelling JANUS Schism does not have. They don't have the imagination for it. Their only appetite is for destruction and dominance. Dominance at all costs."

I looked beyond him to the forest outside. The trees were redwoods in this section: tall, vertical, and what passed for sunlight filtering through in rays. A bird flew by, too quick for me to identify. I could walk for hours in the forest. I was two weeks in the fortress when I could name every fern and flower and weed, creating in my mind a microcosm of words from this microcosm of a biome, containing it, being contained by it, disappearing into it . . .

"Rubak?"

He looked at me.

"Where are we?"

He didn't understand my question at first. Then it dawned on him that I didn't mean this room, this building, or some metaphorical description of our relationship to each other.

"No one ever told you where we are, geographically?"

"No."

It had been kept a secret from me for the whole two years I had been there. I even preferred it that way as it helped me imagine that I'd disappeared for good from the world, that the forest was the entire universe, and everything that had happened to me in the outside world was just a bad dream.

But I also knew the actual dream was the fortress, and I would have to wake up someday. Something told me that today was that day.

"I understand the reason for it, of course," I went on. "Who knows if I'm an agent who will launch a beacon once I know our location? It's unlikely that I am, but the possibility exists, and the risk of it far outweighs the need to satisfy my personal curiosity. I'm an Eve, I know what it means to sacrifice for the team. I was programmed to do so. But I would very much like to know where we are, meaningless as such desire may be. Or to be exact, to know what it is like outside. Is it a forest like this one? Is it a desert?"

A hint of amusement broke through Rubak's tired face. "But such knowledge will tell you nothing about yourself. It's of no importance if you know where you are or not. It is not a knowledge of your inner self."

I let silence settle over the three of us for a moment. He almost convinced me. He wasn't incorrect; if you ever want to convince someone of a lie, mix in a little bit of truth. Then, your listener will be confused, unsure of what part is lie and what part is truth.

But clarity prevailed, and with it, desire.

"I still want to know," I said.

Melesse looked at Rubak.

He stood up. "Follow me."

He led Melesse and me to the fortress wall. When he touched it, an opening into a chamber appeared. We stepped inside, and the aperture contracted into a smooth wall behind us.

The chamber was an elevator. I felt it moving rapidly up, up, up through the walls of the fortress. Was it going to burst out into the middle of the deep ocean? Would the elevator surface upon the sands of a burning desert? Or an abandoned city, with jungle growth overtaking the skyscrapers, using the elevation of the crumbling towers to stretch toward the sun, more sun, and even more sun, to more energy, to more life?

The elevator slowed to a stop and its walls turned transparent.

It took a few moments for my eyes to adjust to the dim almost-darkness.

At first, I thought it was indeed a hot desert at night. Dust blew across wide expanses, and the horizons were as empty as the Taklamakan or the mighty Sahara. But in the distance was something familiar, a thing I thought I would never see again. A herd of them, huddled together against the dark.

Penguins. The dust was not dust but ice. We were in a desert, but not a hot one.

We were in Antarctica.

"I see," I said, staring into the landscape before me. "This is where we are."

Rubak nodded.

"And they are massing here? The Eves?"

"They will be here in a matter of days."

The penguins hardly moved. I wondered if they were frozen in place. "Shouldn't we at least evacuate?"

"Where would we go?" Melesse looked up at her father as she interpreted these words.

I protested, "But there must be some kind of plan, if only an evacuation plan."

"There is no evacuation. There is nowhere to go. We are surrounded."

"Then we have to defend the fortress."

"There are too many of them."

"Then we have to blow ourselves up!"

Rubak smiled.

I persisted. "But don't you agree? You know we can't let all of our technology, our archives fall into the hands of JANUS! It would make the other fortresses . . . how many there may be out there . . . even more vulnerable."

"I admire your thinking. Ethiopians have a saying: those who have no shame have no honor. Shame and honor are very different things, but to us, they have the same weight. The weight of morality. You understand that saving ourselves for the sake of our future and destroying ourselves for the sake of others has the same weight."

"Then why won't you agree with me? Why are we choosing to do nothing, which surely is of lighter weight than fighting back or self-destruction?"

"Even here in Antarctica we aren't safe, where would we run? It is also not our choice to destroy the fortress, if it is indeed possible to truly destroy any nanite being. It's the nanites' choice. For all we know, the entire fortress will simply Rapture and come back a hundred years later. Or clone itself to exist somewhere else. But we cannot destroy the fortress. The fortress has its own destiny, and it is not up to us to intervene in its plans."

"Are you saying the fortress will always provide for us?" A slight barb of cynicism.

"No. The fortress may care very little about us. We have always had the impression that we live within it only because it allows us to."

"You mean, as it did not build itself for us, it does not exist for our sake. If anything, we exist for it."

He nodded, listening to Melesse's translation. "Correct."

"But what about Melesse? What about the Amharic language?"

He closed his eyes and rubbed his temples. He said nothing. The penguins huddled closer together as complete darkness fell over the icy landscape and all we could see were the stars.

As I left the Room of Languages and entered the forest, following the firefly robots that lit my way home, I heard Melesse calling my name from behind.

"May I walk with you for a bit?"

"Of course."

Melesse rarely talked to me or anyone. She was an attentive interpreter, always seeming to disappear into the background, dressing neatly but plainly, her large eyes on her small, round face moving from speaker to speaker as if she was reading their lips as well as listening to their words for her interpretation.

"Do you think I'm a good daughter, Delta?"

"What do you mean?"

"Never mind. You wouldn't know what I mean. I'm sorry, I don't say this as a slight. Perhaps I don't know Eves very well." She sighed. "Sometimes I feel as if my task uses up my language and I have none left for myself at the end of the day. It is so *difficult* to try to say what I intend."

I stopped walking and she slowed down next to me. Standing in the middle of the forest path, the fireflies hovering around us providing their soft illumination, I looked into Melesse's face and waited for her to speak.

"You know how we came to the fortress, Delta?"

I nodded. Melesse's mother had been left behind when Rubak and Melesse had fled west from Addis Ababa, which had been the last human stronghold that we know of to fall in East Africa. Rubak had been a pilot and managed to steal a plane. Melesse's mother had failed to turn up at the rendezvous point, and the carnage was such that Rubak was forced to leave without waiting for her. He flew them as far as a refueling point in South Africa where their plane was hacked into during flight by the nanites of our fortress, guiding it to the fortress's location in Antarctica. The fortress had brought them home.

"We never understood why the nanites brought us here to the fortress. We don't know their plan. Maybe we were just lucky. But I've wondered for years why we were saved and not my mother. We still don't know what happened to her, whether she's alive or dead. And as long as we don't *know*, we can pretend that she's still out there, waiting for us. Maybe she made it to another fortress, who knows? Who knows how many survivors are out there. And that's as far as I let my imagination go when I think about my mother."

"Why are you telling me this?"

"I'm a good daughter, Delta. I care about my parents, just as they care about me as their child. I understand why Father feels defeated. He feels guilty for having left my mother behind in Addis. It eats at him. He can't enjoy his survival, his comfort here. He can't bear to see me grow, knowing that she may never . . . Not to mention all the years they would miss together."

I said nothing. Melesse had never spoken so many words to me before, nor to anyone else other than her father, I suspected.

"But his guilt blinds him to the fact that this is our home now. This is our family. And if we fail to defend it, we'll only end up leaving more people behind."

"Melesse, I don't know what I can do about that."

"You were a soldier once, weren't you?"

I took a step back. "Yes, I killed many people. But I'm not that person any—"

"Soldiers aren't just killers, Delta. They defend what's important, too. Please." She stepped toward me and grabbed my hand. "You have to talk to the other Eves. Convince them that this fortress is worth fighting for. Maybe this is why the fortress brought them here in the first place. It found us, my father and I, and it found you and your friends as well. It needed us. A pilot, an interpreter, soldiers. Please, Delta."

I looked down at our hands, her fingers gripping mine.

I called a meeting of all the Eves in the fortress the next evening.

Not all of them came, and not all who came were Eves. Ellen sat in the back row, not interfering with the proceedings but seemingly watching everything from behind her blindfold, calm and detached. *Icily regular, splendidly null.* From somewhere, that line of poetry came back to me as I glanced in her direction.

My proposal was simple: to determine whether the Eves should step in and help defend the fortress from what looked like an upcoming onslaught. There were many reasons to not do it and few to do so.

The Eves spoke out and over one another, all at once.

"There are too many of them and not enough of us."

"They may not be expecting us. We still have the element of surprise."

"There's no guarantee that they will be surprised. For all we know, every AWOL Eve is suspected to be here in this fortress, an assumed traitor. They might even know exactly how many we are."

"We can't just sit here and wait for them to come and cancel us. We can't let them harm the Redundants."

"What have the Redundants ever done for us?"

"They let us in here and did not kill us."

"She's right. It's their trust that made us human, and our trust that keeps us human."

"Would you rather be human than alive?"

"I would. I was not alive before. I was made alive here. And I'm not going back to what I used to be before."

"Speak for yourself. I say we run."

"There's nowhere to go."

"The ones who want to take their chances should take their chances."

"Not if it compromises our location even faster than it need be."

"If we're not allowed to leave, we are not free."

"Maybe none of us truly are. Maybe none of us were meant to be free. Maybe some things mean more than being free."

"I don't want to die! I want to live."

Our words kept going round and round in circles, and we were never going to arrive at a consensus. Despite our similarities, every one of us was just too different from one another. Only one variation was necessary to make an individual. Not even cloning meant that any two Eves would end up being the same.

Then Eudaimonia, once known as Eve E, stood up.

She stood even taller than before. That was the thing I noticed about her. Perhaps she had been subtly trying to hide her height this whole time, trying to avoid the gaze of the JANUS spies, trying to fit in. But now she didn't hide her height. If anything, she accentuated it, wearing a black suit that was like a sleek sheath holding a thin steel blade.

"We don't do the right thing because we're going to die. We do the right thing precisely because it's the right thing. There is no other reason."

The Eves fell silent. Eudaimonia nodded at me and sat down again.

I addressed the Eves once more. "I propose the formation of three battle units led by me, Eudaimonia, and Aleph. Gia will direct the three of us from within the fortress. Aleph's unit will be with Gia and serve as the last line of defense. Eudaimonia and I will defend the fortress from the outside."

The Eves were silent. Many, however, were nodding, already accepting my orders, my command.

Eve B—who for the past two years still fretted over choosing a name—sat in one of the back rows. She was nodding, and when she saw me looking at her, she gave me a grim and determined smile, sending me courage. Just like that Eve had done on my first evening in the fortress.

It worked. I took a deep breath.

"All right, then. Who's with me?"

Gia, Eve B, and I lay on our stomachs in the frozen trenches, looking out occasionally at the ice plains in front of us. Antarctica was now deep into its six months of night. Our thermals generated heat, and it almost felt cozy in the trenches, although it was unsettling to be in battle mode after two years of complete peace.

"Do you think we'll survive the battle to come?" said Eve B suddenly, as if tired of the quiet.

"Probably not," I said truthfully. "There was something I was talking to Melesse about. Dying is tragic, but I don't want to live with the guilt of not having done everything I could do. Every one of us has enough guilt to last the rest of our immortality."

Gia nodded. "It's one of the things they say around here. The only way to change the past is to change the future. It's the future that matters."

"Even if that future means none of us will live on," said Eve B, "and no one will remember us anymore or the stand we took or what we tried to keep alive. No one will know this conversation happened or the language we spoke to have it."

After the battle, would there still be language here? I looked out into the dark, vast emptiness beyond. What would that language sound like? The words would be different, but the meanings might be the same . . .

"Eve B," said Gia presently, "why haven't you chosen a name for yourself yet? Do you like being Eve B?"

Eve B sighed. "I haven't found a good name yet. Nothing that starts with B feels right to me."

"It doesn't have to start with B," I said.

"I know. But I would still like for it to. I want to be in the same unit as you guys, forever. Aleph, Christina, Delta, and Eudaimonia. Just like the way we started when we got here."

Gia nodded. "A name is nothing if it doesn't connect you to a community. I named myself after my lover. It was her secret name. She was canceled by JANUS."

"I'm sorry," I said.

Gia nodded again, and we lapsed into silence.

The infrared showed no sign of an approaching enemy on the horizon. But we knew, from Eudaimonia's reconnaissance missions, that they were out there, lying in wait. For what?

"Maybe it's the weather," suggested Gia. I realized I had been wondering out loud. "Not even the JANUS schism can stand this cold. Humans couldn't survive it, and we out here are barely enduring. They may be waiting out the season."

"How strange to think of Antarctica as having seasons," said Eve B.

"It does, in a way. Nothing like we're used to elsewhere." Gia lowered the visor on her AR helmet again and peered into the horizon. "A landscape of hidden killer clones," she mused.

"So where have you been, Gia?" asked Eve B. "Someone told

me you're a model five years older than me. That's during the height of the major continental battles."

"I've been everywhere," Gia said firmly, precluding any further discussion on the subject. Discussing the past for Eves was always a fraught subject, having killed so much and seen so much of our own deaths in proximity. Some things were simply beyond language.

"Any places starting with a B?" Eve B asked, hopefully. Even Gia had to laugh.

I pointed at the sky. "What's that?"

An infrared flare streaked across the air above us.

"It's Eudaimonia," said Gia. "They're attacking."

Eve B and I looked at each other. "Well, then," said Gia. "Here we go."

Here we go.

The JANUS units began swarming over the ice just as I saw Gia off down the elevator shaft into the fortress.

"Eudaimonia, how many do you see?"

"We estimate six thousand Eve units on foot so far. There may be more, there are still units coming out of their trenches. They're limited in terms of artillery because of the cold. None of their planes could make it this far."

"What's their formation?"

"There's only one formation possible under the circumstances. They're going for a direct invasion via the elevator."

The fortress could disable the elevator, but the Eves could just as easily rappel down the chute. Even if the fortress sealed the chute with nanites, the enemy Eves could simply bomb their way in; nanites were not indestructible. The Eves would always find a way, especially when there were so many of them. And who knew if they had already discerned the locations of the ventilation shafts, which remained a mystery to the inhabitants of the fortress, or of other access points that we didn't know about.

"Cell bombs deployed. Aleph, how long until they settle in the host body?"

"*Minutes, but the longer you take to give us the order to pull the trigger, the better.*"

I made a mental calculation. "We'll give you your minutes. B-wing, fire!"

Explosions lit up the ice plains as the dugouts to the left of me fired their long-range cannons into the sky, the bombs ribboning trails of light toward the ice before impact. The ground shook. Just then we came in range of their guns, and I ordered everyone to take cover as the bullets began raining down against the cover shielding the dugouts.

Eve B's name blinked in the corner of my AR visor. "*They're not using anything other than bullets. Either they couldn't bring heavier artillery in the cold, or the elevator shaft really is the only access point they know.*"

"Then we'll defend the elevator for as long as we can. We have to give the fortress as much time as possible and do as much damage as we can to the enemy before they infiltrate."

"*Don't worry about us,*" said Gia, "*worry about yourselves. They're coming in from all directions now.*"

I swiped through screens on my AR for the bird's-eye view: Eves coming toward the elevator and the circle of dugouts from every direction, like ants converging on the entrance to their hive. "C-wing, cell-bombs, now!"

The cell-bombs arched through the air again and exploded, hailing down what I hoped were still viable nanites. The weather was simply too cold to guarantee if any of our weapons would work. We had barely enough time to come up with a strategy, much less tests.

"Gia, we need to pull the trigger soon."

"Just give it a few more minutes."

"You can't wait until they're down the chute, once they reach the dugouts . . ."

"Just a few more minutes!"

We were being pelted with bullets, our cannons not really having much effect in punching holes through the swarm. There were easily a million Eves heading toward us now.

"Gia!"

No answer.

"Pull the trigger, Gia!"

They were seconds away from the A-wing dugout.

"Gia, *now!*"

I heard a sound like a sonic boom and winced as thousands of Eves suddenly keeled over and fell into the snow as if their souls had left them. The battleground was full of dead bodies, the un-infected ones tripping over them.

And more coming over the horizon.

We knew we could only use this weapon once. The Eves would

quickly adapt, their bodies learning to register the fuse cells as a threat. The newer Eves could do it in a matter of seconds.

"We have to retreat," said Eudaimonia. I knew by *we* she meant everyone else except her and the first line of defense, who was somewhere in the sea of dead bodies.

I spoke into the comm, "Are you hurt?"

Eudaimonia said nothing. That told me everything I needed to know.

"Eve B! Where are you!"

Her voice came over the comm, weak and despondent. *"I didn't even get to have a name."* Her designation in my AR display blinked off—she was gone.

Gia's name blinked on. *"All wings retreat. Down the chute!"*

The fortress Eves rushed to comply, but I paused and stared behind me toward where the first line of defense would be.

What was waiting for me at the bottom of the chute? At best, a life lived forever in the cocoon of a benevolent, kinder version of JANUS, while at worst a rat's death in a dead-end trap. And while one may be better than the other, what is the weight of that difference, really? *Those who have no shame have no honor.* Whether a life ends happily or sadly, what does it matter but the weight of the emotions one felt, the weight of the clarity of all the meaningful moments one possessed while living on this Earth, whether they have been good or bad? Is it not the weight, in the end, that really makes us human after all?

We don't do the right thing because we're going to die. We do the right thing precisely because it's the right thing.

Instead of going down the chute, I turned, and charged toward enemy lines.

I found Eudaimonia, miraculously still alive underneath an Eve whose face had been half-blown off from the spontaneous apoptosis event. The sight was so horrifying it knocked the breath out of me.

Eudaimonia was almost certainly fatally injured. She looked as if she had staved off the attack of ten Eves at once.

I tried to make her as comfortable as possible.

"Delta . . ."

"Yes. It's me. I'm here."

"Why are you here." She didn't have the energy to make it a question. It sounded like a lament. *Why did you not take the chance I gave you, the life I gave you.*

"I'm here. I'm just here, Eudaimonia."

"You shouldn't be."

"Shh."

"They're coming. So many . . . of them . . ."

"Stop worrying about them. Stop worrying about me. Stop worrying about anyone else from now on."

"Delta . . ."

I thought she was trying to tell me something, but when I looked in her eyes, she was gazing off over my shoulder. I followed her gaze.

But I had felt it before I saw it. A great rumbling, a cracking like thunder. The world coming apart underneath us.

Rising in the dark was a white monster, impossibly large, impossibly familiar . . .

"Oh my God, Eudaimonia, it's the fortress."

I couldn't fathom how long it had taken to gather enough energy from the hot depths of Earth's crust to enable this plan of action—this hidden, stupendous escape plan—how many long hours of nanite thought or whatever passed for nanite thought to find a way to defy gravity and rise, rise, and sail into the stars . . .

Eudaimonia and I stared as the great oval sphere, with its many dangling tentacles, no doubt the cables that had reached into Earth's mantle, rose and rose, slow to the eye but in truth at a rapid rate, until it was another star in the sky.

The other Eves never came back for us, nor for any of their own dead.

They retreated. Eudaimonia died not long after in my arms, too damaged to be regenerated. I buried her, blasting through the frozen soil, and made a kind of camp among the dead near her grave and prepared to join her.

A delta in mathematical notation means change.

Each individual is a delta of its species. A delta of its narrative. Once we stop changing, we die.

No—even the dead change. Because nothing ever dies. Everything lives on in some way. It could be in a very small way, but every action, every word uttered, it changes the universe. It must. Once I finish writing in this notebook, I will lie beside Eudaimonia's grave and recite to myself all the poems that have come back to me, every piece of language that I can remember. And every poem that I recite will be changed because of the fact that I recited it. Because that is what happens to poems. Even if there is no one here to listen to me, the poem will have changed. For even the same poem, recited seconds apart, cannot be the same. It is a different poem every time. We change the poem every time.

I will keep changing and changing and changing the poem, the universe, until I finish hemorrhaging energy into this long night of the Antarctic winter. The sun will not rise in time for us to regenerate, but the poems will not die. After my death, they will ride the web of language entwined with the cosmos and be reborn elsewhere, in other forms. Where, and what, will I be then? I look out into the dark expanse again and imagine a time when all of this has changed. The continent has drifted to a warmer latitude and the land is verdant with forests and plains. There are unimaginable animals. Perhaps even a kind of people.

Which is why I wanted to complete my record of this battle and finish my calling as an archivist of the Room of Languages. So that Eudaimonia and all the fallen Eves, even the JANUS ones in this field, will not be forgotten when in some warmer future, someone comes across this landscape where we will return again, decayed recursions, dead corpses that supposedly tell no tales.

We shall tell our tale, for anyone who cares to listen hard enough.

Read this and know who we were. This record contains all that was meaningful to us. It contains the very weight of our lives. We found not only happiness and sadness and hope and despair but meaning. We leave the weight of it here.

I am Delta. And I was here.

Because I could not stop for Death—
He kindly stopped for me—
The Carriage held but just Ourselves—
And Immortality.

We slowly drove—He knew no haste
And I had put away
My labor and my leisure too,
For His Civility—

We passed the School, where Children strove
At Recess—in the Ring—
We passed the Fields of Gazing Grain—
We passed the Setting Sun—

Or rather—He passed Us—
The Dews drew quivering and Chill—
For only Gossamer, my Gown—
My Tippet—only Tulle—

We paused before a House that seemed
A Swelling of the Ground—
The Roof was scarcely visible—
The Cornice—in the Ground—

Since then—'tis Centuries—and yet
Feels shorter than the Day
I first surmised the Horses' Heads
Were toward Eternity—

CHRISTINA

What I remember of my dreams is the light.

They say you don't dream when you're in suspended animation.
Perhaps they're right. Perhaps what I saw and felt during my time
being archived was not exactly what you would call a dream. Perhaps dreams are only experienced by humans and not clones or
instantiations of some artificial blueprint. Instantiations like me.
But I don't know what else you would call that light. The memories of that light.

> *Those shadowy recollections,*
> *Which, be they what they may*
> *Are yet the fountain-light of all our day,*
> *Are yet a master-light of all our seeing;*
> *Uphold us, cherish, and have power to make*
> *Our noisy years seem moments in the being*
> *Of the eternal Silence*

—

I was unarchived on an Easter Sunday.

That fountain-light was already receding into memory, replaced by a harsher white light that stung my eyes.

I saw the shadow of a head.

My eyes adjusted, and a small, exquisite face of a young African woman came into focus. She looked down upon me like an angel or a surgeon.

"Can you hear me?"

Yes, I wanted to say, but my voice was still waking up. I managed to blink twice instead.

"You're in what used to be called the fortress. It is now called the ark, and we are in orbit of Earth. You've been archived for a long time. Do you remember your name?"

Christina. Christina is a good name.

I blinked twice again.

"Good. That's always a good sign. Normally we don't have trouble unarchiving Eves, but no one has been reanimated after this long a suspension before. Take your time to adjust."

The feeling in my body was slowly coming back to me, as if my brain were struggling to remember every part of it all at once: yes, you have arms. Yes, legs. Yes, the tips of your fingers, the ends of your toes, your lungs drawing breath. Yes, your brain. All these domains are yours.

"We've found and disabled your detonation trigger."

Relief.

"Out of an abundance of caution, we swept your entire nano-self but found no remaining weaponry in your cells. We will keep you in observation for a few days just to make sure." She paused for a moment before saying, "You are also something of a . . . very old model. There's a lot of systemic entropy built up in you that—"

"Delta."

My brain had drawn her name from the depths of oblivion and pushed it forth from my lips.

"Delta?" Another pause. "Concentrate on feeling better, first."

I had the feeling that I needed to calm down if I wasn't going to irrevocably damage myself in the process of waking. The news that my neurological system had been completely swept through while I was under explained why my memories felt strange to me, even though technically it should make no change in how I feel. I felt a mixture of relief and resentment, even when I had to admit that it had probably been necessary toward solving the problem of the self-destruct trigger. I was their prisoner of war after all, for them to do what they will.

The young woman frowned as she looked at something just beyond the top of my head. "Christina, I'm going to put you back into the regeneration capsule. No need to be alarmed, just let the light do its work. Close your eyes."

I closed my eyes.

I spent two more days in regeneration.

I was only conscious for about an hour of that time, with the same young woman asking me to lift an arm, move a toe, or turn my head. Something to do with calibrating my body's motor responses to my brain.

On the third day, I woke up again to the voice of the young woman, only this time she was not with me. Her voice came from outside the room, through a speaker.

"Christina, it's me again. Blink twice like last time if you can hear me."

I blinked twice but closed my eyes again to the light.

"Good. We're just going to do some final exercises to make sure your voluntary motor functions are normal. We'll start with your hands, work our way up, and then down again. How does that sound?"

I blinked twice.

"Good." I heard the soft chimes of buttons being pushed, input being acknowledged. "I'm Afia, by the way. I'm the current head archivist at the Room of Languages. Maybe you know my great-great-grandfather Rubak?"

I vaguely recalled him, the tall Ethiopian and his daughter, standing across from us at the council meeting.

"You must have many questions," she went on, her voice light and cheerful. "I looked up the date of your being archived. That was exactly a hundred years ago. You arrived only a few years before your fortress left Antarctica, the same fortress my great-grandmother Melesse and her father lived in before it merged with the ark. That fortress was really important, it's the one that had copies of the notebook. Codex Mali. An ur-text of both the Redundants and the Immortals."

I remembered the black notebook. Delta had mentioned it in our last conversation before I was archived.

Delta. Where was she?

"Try moving your left hand."

We made our way through my body like she said: hands first, then my wrists, my arms, my shoulders, my head, my face. Then down my torso to my legs, feet, and toes. My body responded to me, there was no miswiring, and as uncomfortable as I felt, I did not feel sick or wrong. I felt like me.

"Oh, I made some more inquiries into that Eve unit you mentioned, the one named Delta. I'm sorry, but it looks like she never made it off the planet during the Great Migration when all the fortresses left Earth. She died fighting off an attack from JANUS. She was a hero."

So they'd left her there in that icy desert. They left her in Antarctica.

They. The nanites.

The nanites that held us here, floating in space.

Afia finally took me out of regeneration. The glass capsule that had contained me was one of many lining the walls and ceilings of a tube-shaped corridor, white and brightly lit, the Eves themselves bathed with light so bright they hurt my eyes. Afia supported me for my first few steps out of the archive capsule, but soon enough, I was able to walk on my own.

We emerged from the underground of the Eve archives into a luscious subtropical meadow.

The first thing I noticed about the ark was its grand curve, the arc of the ark. Unlike the *Ayutthaya* had before it, the ark's "crust" somehow generated its own gravity, enabling the entire inner surface to be populated, the forests planted, the seas, lakes, and deserts tranquil, and the people—I am told a combined total of one million souls—from floating into chaos.

A nanite sun shone in the middle of the hollow sphere, darkened every "night" by a shrouding nanite swarm. It was powered by some kind of nuclear fusion process, learned from one of the other nanite fortresses that had merged with the ark, to combine resources and populations.

A world of both nanites and nonnanites, in fragile symbiosis.

The nanites were now Godlike, they saw everything that they had made, and—behold!—it was very good.

"Where are you taking me now?"

"To your debriefing."

"Debriefing? Am I still a soldier?"

"Not exactly. There *is* a mission. Someone will explain everything to you at the debriefing."

"What happens if I don't accept this mission?"

"I don't know. That hasn't been discussed. But we've a feeling you'll accept."

We.

We walked down a path in the hot sunlight, a warmth that felt soft against my skin. A flowering tree had shed white blossoms on the ground. I picked one up. The blossom was as big as my palm, four perfect petals, a faint yellow at the center that brightened into white outstretched petals. It had a subtle, lovely scent.

"What is this?"

Afia looked back at me. "Oh, that? Plumeria. A very common plant at one time. For all we know there aren't any left on Earth."

"No one has been to Earth since the fortress left Antarctica?"

"We've only just figured out how to catch a ride on the harvesters. The nanites wouldn't let us off the ark until recently."

"Harvesters?"

"Smaller arks occasionally bud off the ark and descend to Earth, which we're still orbiting, in search of material. Resources mostly, even air, but sometimes genetic materials. Plumeria was one of the things that were rescued right after the Migration. A lot of what comes back has been too compromised by the radioactivity of the wars."

"Is JANUS still active?"

"We're not sure. But from what we can tell, it is not, and the war seems to have wound down pretty rapidly after we left. Like JANUS finally began giving up."

"There must be something left of humanity down there."

Afia glanced back at me again. "I hope not. It can't be much of a life. Not for a while, anyway."

Maybe that was how the people on Earth felt when they looked up at the ark, I thought, but I did not say this out loud.

We walked in silence until we came to a large wooden deck with some kind of light, translucent fabric hanging over it in artfully arranged patches for shading. The deck overlooked a vast forest and the gently ascending curve of the ark.

People of all ages and coloring sat about the chairs of the deck, enjoying the light breeze and watching the children play. Surprisingly, an Eve in our old JANUS combat gear sat among them, incongruous and alone at one of the tables, leaning her elbows against it as she looked off into the distance.

"We're here," called out Afia.

She turned. I recognized her at once.

It was Aleph.

"I'm sorry for staring," said Aleph as I sat down. "You look so much like her. Like Delta."

All the Eves looked like one another. But I knew what she meant. Some twins resemble each other more than other pairs, even if their genetic material was identical. For example, Aleph and I didn't really resemble each other. And we were now more distinct from each other than ever before.

"Aleph. Have you been living here for the past century? Your armor must be ancient by now."

"No. Not really. I was archived about ten years after the Migration. I'd had enough of life and crushing guilt. I told them to wake me up when it was another world. But I was unarchived a month ago and the world seems the same to me."

"Not quite the same. So, this is all new to you as well." I swept my arm toward the curve of the ark.

"I was waiting out the deluge of time, just like you. They told me they found your trigger."

"Is anyone going to tell me why I've been unarchived now?"

Afia said, "There's an expedition. An expedition to Earth. And we want you to be a part of it."

I looked out at the light, the pleasure of the sound of children playing, something, I realized, I had never before heard until this moment. It had been difficult for children to stay alive in the war. I tried not to think about that.

Perhaps dementia and forgetfulness were a blessing. No living thing, even an Immortal, could simply keep living and accumulating memories, scars, and trauma. At some point, it was too much. One had to ask to be archived and woken up when there was a new world. A new past.

Or never.

I turned to Aleph. "As far as we know, Earth is a radioactive wasteland with the occasional hostile, but Afia told me she had a feeling that I would accept this mission. Do you know what she means by that?"

"I do. We're going back for Delta."

I felt a wave of unfamiliar emotion at Aleph's words. Something akin to sadness, but urgent. Unexpected.

I took a deep breath and said, "She can't still be alive."

"Then we're going back for her body. But she could still be alive. We know from the comm records that Eudaimonia and Eve B were killed, but Delta was alive to the end."

"That was ages ago."

"She is an Immortal, she might still be alive. If JANUS caught her, she could've been archived. She could still be waiting for rescue. We just left her there."

You did, I thought, but I didn't say it out loud. It was clear to me that Aleph had spent a lifetime regretting what had happened during that battle. She had spent ninety years being archived just to run from the guilt.

"At the very least," she said, "we have to recover her body. The battle was in Antarctica, there must be something still left of them in the ice."

"But why? What's the point? She's made of the same nanites as we are. What makes *her* body special?"

Aleph looked very tired. "If I have to explain that to you, then there's no point in you going. We might as well put you back in the archive."

It was true. I knew why we were going.

"Bringing Delta's body back isn't going to bring her back," I said.

"I know. She won't be the same, even if we do succeed in regenerating her. But—"

"She *won't* be the same. Even by your own admission she won't be the same." I could not stop the words from coming out of my mouth. "And you won't feel less guilty for abandoning her."

"We did not abandon her."

"But you *feel* like you did. You feel like you left her behind to die. You feel responsible for her death."

"I am not responsible for her death."

"No, you're not. But that's not how you *feel*. You want to take responsibility for it because you think it'll bring her back. This is your way of trying to change the past. To bring back your sense of control over what has happened. But you can't control the past. You can't change it. You can't change what the nanites did. Or bring back all the time that has flowed between now and this Great Migration Afia mentioned. Bringing Delta back from the dead will make no difference to that. Bringing her body back from her grave of ice isn't going to change that."

Aleph whispered, "We just left her there. We left all of them there."

"The nanites left them there."

Aleph began to sob. But I knew these weren't tears of sadness. They were tears of relief.

"Aleph," I said, gentler this time, "you have to let go. Maybe even forget. Write over those memories, ask the nanites to do that. You can't keep going back to them over and over again. It won't change what happened and it will destroy your future."

Afia said, as if quoting something, "The only way to change the past is to change the future."

"But how do I change the future? How?"

I glanced at Afia, who looked stricken. Her shock was my own in that moment. I'd known Aleph only briefly before my archiving, but even I knew how strong and confident she seemed from the outside.

But sometimes, the hardest of appearances hide the softest of vulnerabilities. Perhaps even more so.

"We honor them through our living," Afia offered. "We create lives that they would be proud of us for having."

How young she was, how clear-minded. And, how naïve. But I could only nod in agreement, hoping it would be enough for Aleph.

"But that's not all," said Aleph, composing herself. "I don't know how to say this . . . I want to know."

"Know what?"

"I want to know the rest of her story. If it ended, I want to know how it ended."

I sat back. There was nothing I could say to that. Wanting to know what happens next is the most primitive, the most fundamental of human desires, and I had felt it myself when we were investigating the crash site at Tierra del Fuego. I had felt it on the path to this deck as I trailed Afia through the plumeria and the light. And I was feeling it now.

The narrative in this notebook, told over hundreds of years and through the words of many different individuals, constitutes a single story. We belong to it, it does not belong to us. None of our stories belong to us.

What is DNA but lines in a narrative of our lives? What else is all our code? Our literature? They exist before we do. We exist to perpetuate them. To perpetuate story. We are mere vehicles. We tell a story with our bodies, our lives, then we die.

The story lives on.

I rested my hands on the table before me. "When do we leave?"

"Air is notoriously hard to produce artificially," said Afia months later as we settled into our seats in the capsule moving through the "crust" of the ark toward the harvester. "Air as in atmospheric gas itself, not just gaseous oxygen or carbon dioxide. It's still easier to bring air from Earth. Some things the nanites are good at, some they haven't figured out a way to do so well yet."

I adjusted my padded jacket underneath the seat harness as I said, "You make it sound like the nanites have laboratories and do experiments and publish studies."

"I'm quite serious," said Afia. "One of the things we study in the Room of Languages is the nanite language. They've invented a language to speak amongst themselves, they use it to communicate and create. It's a mishmash of human and machine language. Nothing reminds us more than their language of the fact that the nanites come from us. It's human and not human at the same time."

The nanites have their own language.

By this time, I had my own copy of Codex Mali—Delta had reportedly taken the original to the battlefield and we can only presume it is lost forever—and had read through it, just to understand the narrative that I came from and the narrative I was about to contribute my own branch to, perhaps my life to. There was much talk about language. Sometimes, it seemed like the authors were treating language like it was its own creature. A creature that fed, grew, died, and was reborn again. Language was not a tool to them, more like an occasionally useful parasite.

Or were *we* its occasionally useful parasites?

I hoped the ark found us useful parasites. The capsule raced through the flesh of the ark, the nanites parting the way and pushing us along.

The Redundant and Immortal scientists of the ark had managed to figure out how to coax the nanites so they moved more or less according to our will, but it wasn't clear how much depended on our will and how much depended on the will of the ark. The inhabitants of the ark had already succeeded in sending a drone capsule along with a previous harvester and for all intents and purposes, the attempt was a success. This would be the first mission with live people. Our ostensible mission was to recover Delta's body and report on the state of the war, but the real mission was to see if a group of living people—Afia, Aleph, and me—could be sent to the surface of the planet and return unharmed.

The capsule began to decelerate.

"We must be here," whispered Afia.

"Why are we whispering?" I quietly asked.

She didn't answer. The capsule turned, and the stream of nanites against the glass canopy above us cleared to reveal a sky filled with Earth.

It took my breath away.

I turned to Afia but she was silently shedding a tear. It occurred to me that she had never been to the planet of her ancestors before, that this was a moment she needed for herself to process. I said nothing to her and turned to Aleph. She seemed indifferent, lost in thought.

We felt a movement, like the capsule was being pushed from behind. "We're moving," I said stupidly, stating the obvious. The capsule was now on the skin of the harvester, a large spherical object that had budded off from the main body of the ark. Our movement was imperceptible at first, but Earth began getting larger and larger until it was clear we were about to fall through space into the planet.

I couldn't believe the speed in which it happened. We entered the atmosphere and saw water, water that was more steel than blue, waves upon waves. I realized we weren't simply moving rapidly down but also forward, quickly approaching a white landmass.

Antarctica.

—

The harvester began to slow its descent.

We landed, and the capsule separated from the harvester and touched down on the surface of Earth. We watched as the harvester, a large white sphere about a hundred times the size of our three-person capsule, rose and went off on its own way, a pristine white bubble oblivious to the three life-forms it had helped bring to the surface of another planet.

"How do we get it back?" I asked.

"There's a homing device in this capsule," replied Afia as she scanned the environmental reports coming in on the panel in front of her. "There doesn't seem to be too much radiation in these parts but just to be sure, let's put on our hazmat suits. JANUS was no stranger to biological warfare. Also, I'm still picking up some odd readings here and there, even on the site of the Last Battle."

"How far is the old fortress's crater?" Where Delta would be.

"An hour away by foot, over that mountain."

Aleph tossed me a hazmat suit.

We walked through the white wasteland toward the mountains in the distance. Despite the bleakness, I couldn't help thinking it was beautiful; the sun was so bright on the snow that I was glad the hazmat suit came with a visor, automatically activating a darkening tint against the light. The air being filtered through the suit was crisp and cold. I checked the radiation readings on my wristwatch: it had dropped to near zero. Had the planet finally healed? Was the JANUS AI defeated, exhausted of its own zealous desire to destroy?

As we approached the foot of the mountain, I had a strange feeling about a pile of rocks in the distance that was covered in snow.

I realized it wasn't a pile of rocks.

"Look! Something crashed here."

Neither Aleph nor Afia tried to stop me as I broke away from them and approached the shattered shell of the . . . what? It was too small to be a harvester, and it looked like no human-made vehicle I had ever seen, although it was true that I had been asleep for the past hundred years and would not be able to recognize much of recent technology.

The hull was too shattered to allow me to discern what its original shape was, other than the fact that it had shattered. Afia approached the pile of machinery with me. As I brushed away some of the surface snow, Afia said, "You don't suppose anyone might have survived this crash?"

"Do you think it came from the ark?"

"Not from *our* ark. We don't know if there are other arks in orbit, but it's likely there are. Maybe this is from one of them."

I glimpsed something in the dark innards of the twisted wreckage. I froze—it was a hand. Or was it a claw? It had mummified, but I could still tell, it was humanoid, but what human had a *paw* of three thick digits that ended in talons . . .

Surely there are other fortresses in this world where the humans and Eves are trapped inside, being eaten alive or torn apart?

Perhaps Delta had been right to make this assumption. Other fortresses, both on Earth and in space, may have had very different belief systems than the nanites of our ark. They could be doing all kinds of experiments, collecting "samples" and creating monsters out of their genetic material. What if one of these monsters had tried to escape some unimaginable breeding program, tried to hitch a ride on a harvester and make it back to Earth?

I shuddered. We had lucked into being part of the nanite strain that found the preservation and evolution of a humane culture to be as essential to the survival of both nanite and human as our genetic material was. Our fates could have easily been different.

Who could imagine the agonies that went on in the other fortresses?

I said, "There's nothing here. Let's go."

Afia nodded—I had no idea if she had seen the claw or not—and we went back to where Aleph stood, silently waiting for us.

We were almost to the summit of the mountain when I began to hear music.

Even among the Eves, I'd always had an acute sense of hearing. I rarely talked and I tried to make as little sound as possible. Having read Delta's first entry in the Codex Mali, I more than recognized the quiet Eve C that she described. Silence had always been my refuge. I only emerged from it when there was something vital at stake.

I stopped in my tracks. The loudest sound was the crunch of Afia's and Aleph's feet on the snow behind me, but I could still tell there was a sliver of something beneath.

I ripped off the headpiece of the hazmat suit.

Afia cried, "Christina, what are you doing!"

I held up a hand to silence her and looked up at the peak.

It was singing to me. A voice both human and not. At first I thought it was just sounds, but it was music. Harmony, melody, rhythm. Soul.

I turned around. "Do you hear that?"

Aleph took off her own headpiece. Her expression did not register curiosity or surprise. She looked as if she had expected to find music on the mountain of an empty continent, a singing peak.

"I hear it."

"The mountain peak is singing to us."

"I don't think it's the mountain."

Reluctantly, Afia took off her own headpiece. The wind whipped through our hair, Aleph's and mine long and black, Afia's curly and a dark shade of brown, soft yet vibrant with energy at the same time.

"It's Mozart," said Afia. "The dice game."

We looked at one another. We started to climb the mountain again.

At the summit, we could finally look down upon the great crater left by the departing fortress, a kilometers-wide depression in the snow, covered over with a century of ice and geological activity.

But that wasn't the scene that made Afia gasp. She instinctively grabbed my hand. Shocked myself at the sight before us, I barely had the wherewithal to squeeze her hand back.

Wordlessly, Aleph began leading us down the other side of the mountain.

—

In the middle of the crater was a structure almost impossible to describe. It towered over us, easily ten times my height.

Was it a sculpture? A solitary artwork installation of randomly conglomerated pipes in the middle of nowhere? It was gray, seemingly made of burnished steel, but its surface texture was too flawless, even up close, to be made up of anything but nanites.

The sound of music was coming from the wind blowing through the many apertures of the pipes and out the equally numerous funnels that seemed to amplify the sound.

Afia said, "It's like an Eolian harp. It makes music from the wind blowing through it, not by an instrumentalist's playing of it."

"An Eolian harp?"

Afia nodded. "It's in a famous poem:

"And now, its strings
Boldlier swept, the long sequacious notes
Over delicious surges sink and rise,
Such a soft floating witchery of sound
As twilight Elfins make, when they at eve
Voyage on gentle gales from Fairy-Land."

Sequacious. Witchery. Elfin. I shuddered again as the poem came back to me in full force as Afia recited it, this poem that I had never heard of before in this lifetime but had in another one.

I opened my mouth and the words came forth:

"And what if all of animated nature
Be but organic Harps diversely framed,
That tremble into thought, as o'er them sweeps
Plastic and vast, one intellectual breeze,
At once the Soul of each, and God of all?"

I met Aleph's gaze. She was looking at me with that same expression as before, when we were listening to the music from the mountain.

"Aleph, you need to tell us what you know."

Afia looked at me. "What do you mean?"

"Yes, Christina," said Aleph, her eyes still on me. "What do you mean?"

"You knew what we would find here."

"I knew we would find *something* here. I was hoping to find Delta. But instead we found Mozart. Or Ellen. One of those organic harps diversely framed."

Afia turned to the Eolian harp, shielding her eyes from the sun. "The nanites that were left behind must've become this. The ones undamaged by the cell bombs. What was left of Delta and Eudaimonia and maybe even some of the JANUS Eves. They coalesced over a hundred years into this. So maybe you found Delta after all."

Aleph nodded but said nothing. An uncomfortable silence flowed before Afia said, "Right. I'm going to go inside it and take a look around. See what makes it tick."

"I'll go with you," said Aleph flatly, in a tone that preempted refusal. Afia nodded, and they both walked into one of the wind tunnels.

I sat down on the snow.

I had no desire to see what had become of my sisters. I did not want to hear their souls singing the morbidly bright measures from the Mozart Dice Game. I put the hazmat headcover back on, but the music still seeped through. Through the visor I gazed out at the ice shelf and sky beyond the Eolian harp, the six-month summer sun making the white of the ice glint and sparkle. Like an empty page full of the promise of the intimacy of writing, right before one sets down a pen to paper. Writing is a public act, but is there ever a more private one? Could there ever be a more delicious sensation than the intimacy with the page, a better partner in any sin or crime than the white expanses, the undiscovered country, the unspoiled future where we can pretend for a moment that there are no Redundants, no Immortals, no echoes from the past, poetic, genetic, nanotechnological or otherwise? But the moment we lift the pen, the moment we use language, laden as it is with the past, with the victors of conquests and the blood of the vanquished, all the ghosts come flooding back, and we drown.

I must've dozed off because the next thing I remember, Afia was shaking me. "Sorry to wake you, you might want to take a look at this." She held a black notebook in her hand, as if my musings had conjured it.

I took it from her and spread it open. It was, as far as I could tell, the original Codex Mali notebook, the one I am writing in now. My eyes hungrily scanned over Delta's writing until I found an instance of my name. *Christina.*

I could feel the tears well. I closed the book.

In my steadiest voice, I said, "Where did you find it?"

"It's all caves in there, opening and closing. I was afraid I'd get trapped but realized it was continuously reconfiguring itself so that the wind would play different measures of music. I found it in one of the upper chambers, like it was put there by someone who wanted it to be discovered."

Delta. She must've put it there somehow. She was likely part of the Eolian harp now, but she knew someone would come for her, so she let the notebook remain unabsorbed, to continue being this notebook, to have it reveal itself when the harp sensed one of us was nearby.

Afia was looking around. "Has Aleph not come out?"

I looked up at her. "I thought she was with you?"

"We were divided by a closing aperture early on. I thought she would be out by now, I was trapped for at least an hour in one of the chambers."

She turned to the Eolian harp and we both stared at the imposing, graceful organic sculpture as if we expected Aleph or Delta to walk out of one of the openings at any minute.

"I was about to summon the harvester."

"We can't just leave her here," I protested.

"We won't. We can set up camp for now, but we don't have enough supplies for more than one more night and day."

"Then we'll wait for one more night and day."

Afia nodded. My grip on the notebook, which I hadn't noticed was white-knuckled at this point, relaxed. I willed myself not to panic. But I couldn't help a creeping suspicion in the back of my mind, and I could tell Afia was thinking it as well.

———

Before we went to sleep that night, Afia sat outside the tent, making notes on her slate, looking up every once in a while at the sky. I wondered what she was glancing at. She saw me looking at her and made a pair of binoculars with her hands and gestured upwards.

I put on my hazmat headcover and looked up at the sky.

The goggles on the headcover automatically adjusted to the light and I saw the sky as it would appear if not for the midnight sun. I gasped.

Formations of swiftly moving lights, streaking across the sky. They weren't comets, for they were making precise orbits and leaving no trail, as if stars in the night sky had come unfixed from the firmament and were spinning round and round the globe, unable to land, unable to break away, perpetually caught in Earth's gravity well.

"They're other arks," said Afia matter-of-factly. "Now we know for sure there are others."

"How many are they?"

"At least a hundred. I'm surprised they don't collide with each other. Or perhaps they do and ours just hasn't yet."

"Is there any way to tell how big the other ones are?"

"I've been doing the math for that. Most of them are bigger than ours. Much bigger."

"Are they all just up there, waiting for the war to end?"

"Or for Earth to recover. There is another possibility."

I turned to her. "What other possibility?"

"We don't call it an ark for nothing. We're constantly theorizing about the intention of the nanites, reading between the lines of their actions, so to speak. We've determined that ours has stored enough energy and resources to attempt a multigenerational voyage out of our system."

I turned back to the sight of the arks streaking across the sky, trying to absorb what she had just revealed to me. A multigenerational journey. The ark was going to another planet, to colonize it, or to offer our genetic and cultural material to another gene pool and culture. To birth new forms of life and civilizations.

To evolve, to survive.

And surely as it has here, there will be Eolian harps, Eves, and poetry coming back from the dead wherever poetry goes, spreading out into the galaxy and beyond, as long as every ark isn't swept into dust by solar winds, meteors, or other violent fates.

But even if the arks did become dust, dust even finer than the smallest survivable nanite, I had a feeling the poetry would never die. Delta was right. The words may die, the grammar and the melody, but not the song, not the noise. Not the living thing that it was. The language, the music was entwined in the very fabric of the universe and every individual was only its knotted bits or scraps of its fibers, balled up in a brief mess that would only come undone once more, like knots disappearing as the fabric smooths, like waves into an ocean.

I did not sleep at all that night. I rose when Afia did. We had breakfast. We did not talk to each other the whole morning. We did not talk through lunch. We simply listened to the faint music of the Eolian harp, which changed its melody according to some engine of random chance, moving from one Mozartian measure to the next.

In the afternoon, Afia finally spoke up. "You know as well as I do that she's not coming back."

I nodded.

"And I'm guessing that you don't plan on coming back with the harvester, either."

I sat still, saying nothing. I didn't know what to tell her.

Afia turned to the Eolian harp. "Do you think she's part of it now?"

"I think that's the likeliest explanation. She didn't want to live forever and she came back here for Delta. And in every important sense, this harp *is* Delta."

"But *you're* Christina. What do you plan to do here?"

I said nothing. Afia understood.

"You mean to join Delta and your sisters. You mean to die."

I said quietly, "It's not a death—"

"Why!" Afia exploded in rage. "Why do you want to kill yourself!"

I began to cry. How was I to explain this to her? That it didn't matter if I went back to the ark or not, that everyone I had ever cared for in my life was now part of that Eolian harp, that I did not want to traverse empty space in a generation ship, to die in it so far away from here, to have such a long and cold expanse to cross after I die before reaching this radioactive, desolate planet that had once been the birthplace of all our poetry, all my sisters . . .

I wanted to join my sisters.

Not even nanites were immortal. But our language was.

"Afia." I wiped away my tears. "Afia. Do you speak Amharic?"

Afia nodded. She turned away from me.

"Do you understand why Rubak kept the language alive? He knew you would exist, even before you existed. You are the reason he kept it alive. Do you understand that this is the gift he gave to you, your place in the story of this language? And this harp is the gift of my sisters. You know in your heart, Afia, that this is how my story has to end. It can have no other ending."

"We can change stories," she said, still not looking at me. "We can change endings!"

I smiled. "I'm supposed to die, anyway. None of us are truly immortal. And I have had a marvelous, marvelous life. I've seen the blue of the ocean in Thailand. I've held the purple disk of a shell in my palm. I've eaten an apple. I've had the love of my sisters. They died for me. I want to . . . I want us all to be reunited. I want us to sing together. They're singing to me. They're singing to all of us to come home."

I do not have much time. I am tired and writing is exhausting me. No, not the writing. The waiting for the inevitable. I can no longer delay the ending of the story, of my story.

I convinced Afia to call the harvester, that she had to leave as we had run out of supplies. That she needed to go back to the ark. She agreed on one condition: that I write down my thoughts into the notebook Delta left behind, that she would take some part of me back to the ark where it would live among the stars when the ark left Earth's orbit someday on its inevitable voyage of generations. I tried to refuse her, but I could not turn Afia back empty-handed, and clearly this was the next part of the story that must go into this notebook. So I have been up all this white night, writing down my story.

And now I have come to the end.

I have given one last look at the ark stars streaking across the sky. Once the Redundants and Immortals scatter across the galaxy, will we still understand one another's languages, millions of years past the point of our last goodbyes to one another? Will the poetry survive?

I think it will.

In some form, I think it will.

It is in the very fabric of this universe, and it will outlast us in the end.

Farewell, and may the stars grant you safekeeping.

PART 4

THE VERY DISTANT FUTURE

MALI

When I come to, there is fog everywhere. Rocks, stones, and trees. And a fog so thick, my skin is soon beaded with it.

Someone nearby, shrouded in mist, is watching me.

"Who's there," I croak.

The shadowy figure approaches. She stops just as her face becomes visible through the mist.

"Who are you," I say, the name an effort on my just-reformed esophagus and tongue.

"We've never met," she replies. "I'm Roa."

"But who are you," I say to her as I sip the brew she handed to me, apparently conjured out of thin air. "You must be more than a name. You must be someone to do with me."

She nods, adjusting a heavy wool blanket over my shoulders, another item that simply and magically appeared in her hands. "I suppose I'm not really Roa, anyway. Just as you're not really Mali. We both Raptured a long, long time ago."

My memory, or Mali's memory, is returning little by little. Mali had been the secret and final radical nanotherapy clinical trial patient before the Beeko Institute was shut down. She then Raptured not long after she gave Panit his nanodroid body. "I'm what came back as Mali. Like Yonghun when he came back."

Roa nods. "The one you called Patient One. Some of us come back. Some of us leave such an echo in the nanite swarm that the nanites bring us back."

"An echo? Of what?"

"Some might call it love." She smiles.

I look out into the fog. "Where is this place? Why is it so misty?"

"Breach in the hull. Some asteroid, all the way out here. A water tank near the collision site quickly converted its contents into steam and vented it into the ship's cavity. I'm assuming the hull has been sealed, it's beginning to clear up."

"We're on a ship?"

She hands me a familiar notebook, the very one I am writing in now.

"A lot has happened since you Raptured."

The fog is clearing, but slowly. It is still heavy by the time I finish reading and could just about discern the faintest "sun" above us, soft and clear. Roa had sat down on the grass nearby, staring off into a nearby forest the entire time I read.

"Where is everyone?" I ask. My voice is finally warmed up,

like my body. The brew, like this notebook, must've been made of nanites. And the blanket, and who knows what rocks, stones, and trees . . .

"They're archived."

"Even the humans?"

"I don't know. I came back only a day before you did. I haven't seen anyone else."

"How do you know the nanobeings are archived?"

"I hear them. Like it says in the notebook, we are all Panit. The Eves, the fortresses, the vats. We're all instantiations of Panit." She grins. "Especially me, because they used his nanites to save my life at one point." She stretches and lies down flat on the ground. "We've had some conversations while I waited for you. They have a lot of questions. I couldn't answer almost any of them."

"What did they ask?"

She shrugs. "What do I remember? What do I think? What do I feel? What is my favorite poem now? They almost sounded like Yonghun in the journal, the one that came back."

"I guess, with you having his nanites, you're the closest thing they have to a parent."

"I would think Yonghun would be that. Or even you."

"Why haven't the nanites brought him back? Why have they brought *me* back?"

"Everyone thinks I have answers. I really don't have any. Not any that matter. I do think . . . They're trying to bring Yonghun back. Everything survives in the echo, and everything comes back. Make sure you write in that notebook before you leave here because it doesn't know how to write itself yet. I know this doesn't answer your questions." She stands up. "Anyway, I have to go now. I've served my purpose. I've repaid my debt to Panit. He did save my life, giving you back this notebook for him is the least I could do in return."

"Where are you—"

She is gone.

When I am not and none beside—
Nor earth nor sea nor cloudless sky—
But only spirit meandering wide
Through infinite immensity.

I hear Bach coming from the forest.

Notebook in hand, I get up and walk into the darkness of the woods. Immediately, insects gather around my head, curious and inquisitive. One lands on the back of my hand. It has eight wings and slitted pupils like a cat. Before I can scream, it flies away.

I think I glimpse an eight-eyed mouse. I can't be sure. Whenever I spot movement, I look away.

I keep walking toward the music.

A structure. Long collapsed in on itself, like an ancient ruin. Built around ancient trees.

Ducking, I enter the gap on the side that used to be an arched entrance. I'm in a clearing—no, an auditorium. A single shaft of light falls on the center of the stage. The strains of Bach fade away as I realize who is sitting there on a rock, her back to me.

I would recognize her anywhere.

—

"Mother!"

The strength leaves my legs, and I collapse as the woman turns around—Nomfundo Beeko. She slowly stands up, the fabric of her gray dress automatically adjusting itself to the fall of her body.

"Mali?" She sounds confused. "Mali, where am I? Where are we?"

Somehow, I know we will not have much time. And it would turn out, eventually, that I'm right.

"Echoes, Mother," I whisper as she helps me up. "We're echoes inside an echo." I hug her fiercely, feeling her being taken aback, and then accepting, finally consoling.

"But whatever do you mean?" she says as I finally bring her to arm's length to look her in the face. She looks so healthy! A young woman, full of intelligence and life and—

"Love, Mother. That's the echo. But echoes are weak, and we don't have much time. The people who were us, the original Nomfundo and Mali, their love for each other was so strong that the nanites, they made us come back, we're like phantom limbs but centuries old, like ghosts—"

"And this place?" She glances about, gripping my hands, firm and sure. "You said this is an echo, too?"

"I don't know, I think only the light and the fog aren't nanites, possibly the dirt. I think everyone living here must've transitioned, we're on a generation ship or something, some sort of interstellar ark—"

"It would make sense to transition, then. To sleep while crossing the vast expanse of space—"

"Mother, I missed you, I've missed you *so much*, I would've given *anything* to have this moment with you—"

My words, and all my language, collapse into sobs, into pure emotion as they lose form. I grip onto her and sense she is already slipping away, already as my words start coming back her reassuring grip feels lighter, lighter . . .

"Mali, I love you."

"Mother, I love you, *I love*—"

She is gone.

The universe still echoes from the Big Bang that created it. Nothing disappears, and everything comes back. Mother will come back. I will come back . . . and yet. The universe is also mostly empty space and time, our own space and time is so brief, and our space and time together briefer still.

But somewhere in the very beginning, everything had been in the same place at the same time, sparking the entire universe to life. It was the beginning of longing, and loneliness, and separation. But Mother showed us there's no such thing as a division between Redundant and Immortal. Immortals are redundant, and Redundants live on in the echo forever.

Like Yonghun before me—the Yonghun in the very beginning of this notebook, the one who came back—I feel the nanites are almost finished with me and I will once more join the fabric, the wake. The echo. I will see Mother again. I am sure of it.

That once I disappear into that fog, she will be there, welcoming me home.

PART 5

ETERNITY-

who

wind

who has seen

has

has . . .

who has seen the wind

The smaller man is the first to arrive.

Arrive is not the exact word. How inexact words are. How rich they are for being inexact. What portals into vast worlds each inaccuracy creates.

He has been there for a long time. He has not been himself for much of that time. He has been himself for only a very small sliver of all of that time.

He arrived, and he thinks he is alone, but he has never been alone.

He has never been less alone than he is now. Which he is about to find out.

He examines his hands. Or his "hands." The knowledge of the nanites had a universe to cross in terms of time, and he is far from being a faithful replication of the original. But because nothing dies and everything comes back, he has come back. Not whole, not as before, but as himself. He has come back.

He tries his voice. It sounds strange against his ears. The air is different now, the atmosphere is not the same as the one he had left. The nanites strain to provide the sensations, they strain against the design they are working from. Some changes had to be made. Not as dramatic as the changes to the other instantiation—the nanites have very little data on him—but then again, even the smallest change has an unexpected impact on the oneself-ness of oneself.

He is himself. Will he keep being himself?

He examines his hands. His "hands."

His brain twists with the memories that are trying to come back. They squeeze into the crevices of what is now an unfamiliar container. The discomfort is incredible. How can anything stand being alive, how can anything stand being on this plane of existence, being itself?

But he knows he has to stand it because . . . of what?

His very consciousness is a mess, unable to think with any clarity, it is drowning as it tries to wake.

Waking itself is a state of being drowned, of deluging those parts that become the subconscious. The waterline of his consciousness creeps up along the burgeoning memories and thoughts, submerging most of them. From here, the nanites negotiate a narrative.

The narrative produces him.

For a moment, his own heartbeat deafens his ears.

His eyes focus. The programming speaks.

Hello, world.

He has no memory of this place. That is correct because he has never been here before.

The landscape is as alien as the air.

There are planets, hugely visible, creating graceful curves in the evening-blue sky. Upon the indigo shading into black farther up the dome of the sky is a scattering of unfamiliar stars.

The earth is red. The horizon is a little farther than the horizon in his memory. Flat, save for a few mesas in the distance. And a strange oval sphere, jutting out of the ground, crashed there perhaps, which must be very large up close but is too far away to seem significant now.

How long are the days here? The years?

How long did he wander the plains of red under the indifferent pockmarked satellite planets taking up the sky, his own skin feeding off the reflected sunlight of their dim primary star?

Time is different on this planet. Elongated, lax, a second lasting minutes, hours, days. There seems to be no day. No matter how long he walks, the light doesn't seem to change.

It is neither bright nor dark, just a pleasant dimness that gives the colors around him—the reds and browns and blacks of the earth, the blues and mauves and indigo of the sky, the thin white and yellow line of the horizon—a deeper hue.

He walks, and thinks he is alone.

At first, he thinks it's his own voice. He thinks it's the sound of his memories returning, for they keep returning.

It is hard to tell whether the memories return before the words or if the words bring the memories with them. If it is the latter, then it is clear the words carry more than just his memories. They carry the memories of others, other individuals and civilizations . . .

Often he pauses to look around to see if someone has spoken, but no one has spoken. It is only the words being resurrected, being spoken in his new mind for the first time. They do not wholly belong to him, if they even do belong to him in the smallest way. They feel Other and yet live within him, like parasites.

Then one day, he hears something that is not himself, that is not the words.

Who has seen the wind?

He turns around, abruptly. There is no one there except the landscape from which he came. The wind blows on his back and he turns again to face it.

Something glimmers there.

Who is it, he thinks.

"Who . . ."

The word comes out as a croak. No one has ever spoken aloud before on this planet.

The glimmering thickens as more motes sparkle.

Soon there is a great flame of copper and silver lights whirling in the air, oblivious to the wind, or creating it.

Never has there been such a thing, on this planet or off.

The smaller man recognizes the taller instantiation. The recognition hits him so hard that it strikes tears out of his eyes.

But no matter. He is running now, toward the light. And soon he will run out of his own narrative, out of the reach of poetry, toward eternity.

ACKNOWLEDGMENTS

First and foremost, my incredible editor Tara Parsons suggested I write additional scenes that are now my favorite parts of the book (also, a big thanks to her son Hunter!). Alexa Frank, Stephen Brayda, Courtney Nobile, Brieana Garcia, and everyone at HarperVia made the most gorgeous book of my dreams. My angelic agent Safae El-Ouahabi along with Jon Wood, Aanya Davé, Sam Coates, Tristan Kendrick, Katharina Volckmer, and Stephen Edwards swooped down and lifted me up out of the waves. Rachel Min Park and Sung Ryu read my early drafts and gave me much needed encouragement. Nicha Suebwonglee suggested that Panit should have a child—whom I almost named Nicha. My grad school advisor, Dr. Nancy Jiwon Cho, taught me poetry and gave literature back to me. Love to the Smoking Tigers, the Null Subjects, the Independent Atelier, the British Centre for Literary Translation, the National Centre for Writing, the Bread Loaf community, and ARMY! Much love to the many authors I translate—Kyung-Sook Shin, Bora Chung, Kim Un, Lee Seong-bok, Sang Young Park, Jeon Sam-hye, Jung Young Su, Sung-il Kim, Baek Sehee, Park Seolyeon, and Djuna. Lastly, this novel would not exist without my husband who nurtured it from acorn to oak. I love you beyond poetry.

A NOTE ON THE COVER

Anton Hur is a cover designer's writer, and *Toward Eternity* is filled with an overwhelming number of cover design opportunities. His descriptions of alien worlds were especially intriguing for me and became the foundation for the final cover.

Lines like "the landscape is as alien as the air. There are planets, hugely visible, creating graceful curves in the evening-blue sky" and foreign forests with flowering trees and their blossoms "as big as my palm" inspired the cover's surreal garden scene. I wanted the cover's landscape to feel as rich as Hur's writing, the plants clearing just enough to invite the reader in.

—Stephen Brayda

Here ends Anton Hur's
Toward Eternity.

The first edition of this book was printed
and bound at Lakeside Book Company
in Harrisonburg, Virginia, June 2024.

A NOTE ON THE TYPE

The text of this novel was set in Carré Noir, a typeface designed by Albert Boton in 1996. A native of France, Boton was working as a carpenter at his father's workshop when, while installing new windows into a city building, he discovered a graphic design agency on the very last floor. His encounter with the designers sparked Boton's interest in type, and he promptly left the workshop to strike out on his own. After attending evening classes at L'école Estienne in Paris, Boton joined several French design agencies of repute. In 1981, he became the head of the type department at Carré Noir, whose name inspired this elegant typeface.

HarperVia

An imprint dedicated to publishing international voices,
offering readers a chance to encounter other lives and other
points of view via the language of the imagination.